T.

By Larry Deibert

Merry Christmas
Noelle

Writers Exchange E-Publishing
http://www.writers-exchange.com

The Other Side of the Ridge
Copyright 2013 Larry Deibert
Writers Exchange E-Publishing
PO Box 372
ATHERTON QLD 4883

Cover Art by: Josh Shinn

Published by Writers Exchange E-Publishing
http://www.writers-exchange.com

ISBN: 978-1-922233-46-2

Acknowledgements

I would like to thank my readers and editors for their input to make *The Other Side Of The Ridge* a well-written novella.

Thanks, Linda Furlow-Patty, my daughter Laura Deibert Beck, and my wife, Peggy Deibert.

I also need to thank Sandy Cummins for publishing my book. She put a lot of time into making this the best book possible.

GETTYSBURG
June 27th, 2013
To
July 2nd, 186

June 27th

1

Dan Rodin felt a stiff breeze tickle the back of his neck. He looked up through the thick foliage and saw the sky rapidly turning from slate gray to black. He figured he had very little time to get inside his shelter. As the wind picked up, he searched for a suitable spot to set up his dome tent to ride out the approaching storm.

A few minutes later, after finding a small clearing in the dense woods, he hurriedly shucked his rucksack, untied the tent, set it up, crawled in, pulling his gear with him, and zipped up the door. Moments later, the wind buffeted the nylon structure from all sides as he pulled his cell phone from his shirt pocket and punched in some numbers.

Three rings later, a voice said, "Sandy Ridge Weather Station. Will Jennings speaking."

"Hi Will, it's Dan. How are you, my friend?"

"Dan! What a nice surprise. I didn't think I'd hear from you until you got back from your quest. What's up?"

"Could you check the radar and tell me how long this storm is going to last?"

"What storm? Where are you? I'm sitting at the monitor as we speak and there is no weather within five hundred miles!"

Dan briefly digested this information, figuring that maybe there was a glitch in Will's equipment. "You sure? I'm buttoned up inside my tent and the wind outside has got to be at least about fifty miles an hour. I could swear a tornado is about to touch down." He looked at his watch. "It's only three o'clock and it's really dark outside."

"Hang on a moment?"

While he waited for Will to come back on the line, a gust of wind hit the tent, lifting one side off the ground momentarily. When it came back down, he was thrown completely across the four-foot wide floor, recoiling off the other side of the shelter.

"Dan, the radar shows absolutely nothing. Can you tell me exactly where you are?"

"Sure. I'm in a wooded area near Chambersburg, Pa., along the route Lee's Army of Northern Virginia marched in 1863. I parked my Forrester on the side of the road. When I started out, the weather was beautiful, but about a half hour after I left the road, I noticed the sky turning gray and it was getting quite windy. A gust just threw me across the inside of the tent, Will. I swear a tornado is going to touch down here any moment, and I have nowhere to hide. I gotta tell, ya, man, I'm really scared. I'm going to ride it out and then I'll..."

2

The conversation abruptly ended. Will was concerned when Dan said he was really scared. Being afraid of a storm after all he went through in the war gave Will cause for concern. He redialed Dan's cell phone twice, but got absolutely nothing. He called his friend, Jim, at Weather Underground. "Jim, do you have any weather showing up on satellite near Chambersburg, Pa.?"

"I'll check." A few moments later, he came back on the line. "Will there was some weather in that area, but it only lasted for a few minutes and then it was gone. Damnedest thing I ever saw. I don't know if I could even explain it, but I have the coordinates if you want me to fax them to you?"

"Yeah, that would be great. Can you send me a copy of the picture as well?"

"No problem, it'll be in your hands shortly. Can I ask you what's going on?"

"Don't know much, but Dan Rodin, an old friend of mine, called me a couple of minutes ago and told me he was sure a tornado was right on top of him. His phone cut out and I can't reach him to see if he's all right. I'm going to try again after I hang up with you."

"You should be able to get him now because the area is clear as a bell. Hope he's okay."

"Thanks for your help, Jim. Talk to you later."

"No sweat. Say hello to Laura and the kids for me."

"I sure will. You do the same with Jane for me."

Will hung up; he dialed Dan again.

3

After he realized he had been cut off, Dan prayed. The wind died down to a slight breeze; but it was raining hard, so he stayed inside the tent. When the rain stopped, he unzipped the tent door and stepped outside. He turned a complete three hundred and sixty degree circle and saw in disbelief that there was no damage at all to any of the vegetation in the immediate area. He did notice that the surroundings appeared quite different than they were before the storm. Odd, but the trees weren't as tall as he remembered. He scratched his head, totally perplexed. The air even seemed to be fresher than he had ever smelled it before.

He went back into the tent and picked up his phone. When he punched in Will's number, a 'No Service' message showed on his screen. He turned off the phone, hoping that he would be able to get a connection later on.

He was ravenous. He searched his pack for an MRE-meal ready to eat-and selected a veggie burger. Since they could be eaten hot or cold, he chose to not heat his meal. He was bone tired and just wanted some fuel to keep him going.

After eating, he walked into the woods to explore a bit and gather wood. He picked up some dry tinder and a few small logs as well. After constructing a fire pit, he created a tepee of branches over a handful of wood shavings he had cut with his pocket knife, and started a fire with one match. As the kindling burned, he added more branches and finally a small log. He took a drink from one of the three canteens he brought with him, and even though the water was slightly tepid and had a plastic taste, the liquid felt good going down his throat.

He sat down on the ground and pulled a small notebook from a thigh pocket of his jungle fatigue trousers. He remembered when they were first issued to him in Vietnam, crisp and so green. After he arrived at the firebase, one of the men he was about to command said, "LT, the gooks are gonna know that you are a newbie lieutenant if you wear them out in the bush. Might be a good idea to find some faded fatigues." Dan loved wearing these fatigues because they had plenty of pockets. He could stuff them with everything he needed for a day hike and leave his rucksack in the tent. He wrote the date, and in a neat penmanship, jotted down the day's events. He had countless notebooks at home filled with information and stories about previous hunts, but this was indeed the strangest entry he had ever made. After transcribing his thoughts about the storm, he put the notebook in his pocket.

From the other large pocket he pulled out the book he purchased over the winter to guide him in his search to find the trail of Robert E. Lee as he moved from Maryland into Pennsylvania, and ultimately, Gettysburg. The compact leather-bound, book, "My March to Glory" by Corporal Andrew Haskins, CSA, cost him five hundred dollars, but the sketches of the terrain could help him immensely in his quest. As he began to read, he fell asleep.

Dan was awakened by the sound of numerous gunshots on the other side of the nearby ridge. It sounded like musket fire and his curiosity was piqued. He stuffed the book back into his pocket, and then looked at his watch: it was nearly six o'clock at night. The fire had gone out and he would have to make another one later. He walked through a patch of woods and climbed up the ridge until he reached the crest.

On the other side of the ridge, he saw an orchard filled with tents. Several men were shooting at targets in the distance. A few men were milling around campfires. The Stars and Bars of the Confederate flag were flying beside one of the tents.

He took his binoculars from a side pocket and lay down to observe the scene more closely. There were hundreds of men in gray and butternut jackets. Some were laughing, conversing. Several men were cooking food on the fires, while others were just resting in the shade of some trees.

Rifles were stacked between the tents. By the tent where the Rebel flag flew, alongside a red and blue flag bearing the letter A--Robert E. Lee's personal flag--was an iron-gray horse hitched to a tent peg. The horse bore a remarkable resemblance to Traveller, General Lee's horse during the Civil War. He smiled and nodded. These re-enactors were really good.

Soldiers who appeared wounded were brought into camp on stretchers, while others walked in, their faces strained, as though they had been in combat. The casualties appeared real, but that, he knew they were-n't. When he heard some twigs snap behind him, Dan quickly turned and stared at two men wearing Confederate gray pointing rifles at him.

"Luke, lookee what we found here. A stinking Yankee spy and he's a nigger to boot."

Dan rose to his feet and barked, "Watch your mouth; calling me a nigger just doesn't cut it!"

Momentarily taken aback by his verbal attack, the two men lowered their rifles, but as he took a step toward them, the rifles came back up once again.

He studied the men. Both were about the same height, perhaps five feet eight inches, although the one named Luke was somewhat overweight for his height. He had apparently not shaved for several days, or more, and his moustache nearly covered his mouth. His steel colored eyes had that 'thousand yard stare'. He wondered if the man had been in combat in Iraq or Afghanistan. The other man had long, black hair that was tied back, and his green eyes were laced with hatred. A few small twigs and leaves were tangled in his beard. Their uniforms looked so authentic that he had to smile.

"What you smiling about, boy? Get that smirk off'n your face before I blow it off!" Luke moved closer and touched his forehead with the tip of the rifle. When he pulled his head back, Luke laughed and looked toward his partner. "Billy Joe, why do you think this nigger was smiling at us?"

Billy Joe shook his head. "Don't know brother, but he sure is one uppity nigger, ain't he?" The two men crudely laughed.

Dan was enraged as they kept calling him that name, "How about we all head down to the orchard and talk to your leader about all this." He was infuriated, but he tried to remain calm, not knowing what these men were going to do to him if he pushed the issue.

Luke lowered his rifle. He circled Dan, looking him over. He placed a hand on his chest, and looked him up and down. "What kind of uniform is that? I ain't never seed Yanks or Rebs wearing green." He pushed him to the ground, and then motioned with his rifle for him to stand up again. "Don't you worry, boy. We sure as hell going to take you down to camp."

Dan smiled again. Apparently these two re-enactors were gonna play out their roles to the hilt. "Okay, I guess I am your prisoner. I'll allow your commanding officer to grill me."

Billy Joe raised his eyebrows. "What does that mean? You'll allow my commanding officer to grill you? You got a name, nigger?"

He had had enough of this charade, thinking that these two guys were truly racists. He was furious. "I'm Brigadier General Daniel Rodin, United States Army."

The two men laughed again and when they stopped, Luke turned toward his brother. "The Yanks must be near scraping the bottom of the barrel making a nigger a general. Shit, we ought to win this war in no time if that be happening."

Dan was tired of the game, but he decided to let it slide until he got into camp. As they walked down the other side of the ridge to the encampment, he asked, "What's your commanding officer's name?"

The men stopped dead in their tracks and Billy Joe replied, "You must be the dumbest general in the Union army, not knowing that you are about to meet Robert E. Lee."

He sounded so truthful Dan started to get worried. "What day and year is this?"

Luke laughed again. "It's June twenty seventh, eighteen hundred and sixty three. We're in Yankee country and we're gonna win this war."

4

As they entered the Confederate camp, Dan walked ramrod straight, his demeanor and gait befitting that of a brigadier general of the US Army. He studied the soldiers, equipment, and tents with intensity, finally believing that he had transcended time and was now a prisoner of war. He rapidly scanned the area, looking for possible avenues of escape.

I am a prisoner of war and I won't even be born for another eighty-six years! Is there a reason I'm supposed to be here because when the storm hit, I was still many miles from here; this place that is no longer an orchard in 2013? There is a simple marker proclaiming that this spot is where Lee set up camp for five days prior to the battle. I remember seeing the marker on some website and this beautiful orchard has become part of the city of Chambersburg.

He gazed at the soldiers staring at him. Faces etched with both hatred and curiosity followed him as he and his escorts strode toward the headquarters tent of Robert E. Lee. He heard numerous catcalls and derogatory insults from the unruly Rebs. Nigger was yelled out more times than he could count and he was now fearful that he might not make it out of this camp alive. The air was filled with flies, feasting on uncovered excrement. This, along with the scents of unwashed human bodies, blood of the wounded, and spoiled meat, plus the smoke from the campfires, and gun oil made him nauseous. However, as he arrived at Lee's tent, he maintained his posture.

Luke briefly spoke to the general's guard, who then went inside the tent for a few moments. When the guard stepped outside, he motioned for Dan to step inside the tent.

5

When the faxes arrived, Will studied the pictures in amazement. He saw a huge cloud formation over the spot where Dan could have set up camp, but in each frame it became smaller and smaller until it disappeared. The storm never moved in any direction, it just shrank! The elapsed time was not more than ten minutes and he couldn't believe that any weather could do what that storm just did. He was totally stumped. He decided to quit work early and take a drive to Dan's location, which was easy to find on Google Earth. He was becoming quite concerned about the welfare of his friend. MapQuest showed it would take nearly two hours to get there. He'd have ample time to look for him before dusk.

He saw the Subaru Forrester parked along the side of Rocky Mountain Road. He got out of his car and checked to see if Dan had returned to the vehicle in the last couple of hours. He wasn't inside, so Will tried calling him. Once again, there was absolutely nothing.

He walked to the wood line and smiled. Dan still had the good habit of marking his trail, so Will figured he'd hook up with his friend in short order. He began to follow Dan's trail.

He found the place where Dan set up camp, but there was no tent, no campfire, no nothing. He shouted Dan's name several times, but did not receive a response. He scratched his head, wondering where his friend had gone.

The area had definitely seen some weather as trees were bent over and pools of water had collected in depressions in the ground. The wet areas spread out about fifteen feet in each direction, almost in a perfect circle, from where he assumed the center of the campsite would have been. Everything outside the circle had not been touched by any type of precipitation or wind. He was totally puzzled.

He stepped on something solid-a Civil War artifact perhaps. He bent down and scraped a little grass away, finding a rusted pocketknife that could have been there for years for all he knew. He pulled a handkerchief from his pocket and began to rub away some of the crud. As the rust loosened up, Will saw the letters LTDAN etched into the handle. This was the knife he gave to Dan back in Vietnam. He was totally baffled. They had been friends for over forty years and he knew that Dan had never searched in this area for Civil War artifacts. He had seen Dan's collection of bullets, brass, cannon balls and uniform buttons. Dan had a map on the wall of his home office showing all the places he had found artifacts, and Chambersburg was not listed; but it made sense, since Robert E Lee's army bivouacked here for a few days before moving into Gettysburg. That he knew for an absolute fact after reading that book by one of Lee's soldiers. He still had to smile recalling how he razzed Dan about how much he paid for that book. How could this knife be here when he never visited the area before? Not only that, but if this was his first visit and he dropped his knife, how could it appear to have been lying on the ground for years? Will was confused and he was also becoming very frightened about his whereabouts. He took out his cell phone and punched in a number.

"Hello?"

"Harry, its Will. I think something bad has happened to your brother, and I don't know what to do."

"What happened?"

He told him about the phone call, the freak storm, the photos, and his trip to Dan's campsite. "...When I found his pocketknife, I had no clue what to make of it, except that I know he would never let it out of his sight. I gave it to him that day at Xuan Loc after the battle, remember?"

"It's something I'll never forget. If he hadn't taken out that gook machine gun, you and I wouldn't be around to talk about it. Hard to believe that was over forty-three years ago, when it seems like yesterday."

"I know. When I rubbed the crud off the knife and saw LTDAN, I felt a chill go up my spine. What I don't understand is that the knife appears to have been lying on the ground for who knows how long. He has only been out of contact for a few hours."

"You're sure that you checked out every possibility? You know how he gets when he's relic hunting."

"Yeah. I know he can really get wrapped up when he's out hunting, but there is no way he's around here now."

"Listen, man, I can come down to Sandy Ridge tomorrow. I'd like to take a look at those photos too. There has to be some logical explanation to this."

"Okay, I'll see you tomorrow. I want to look around some more before I pack it in."

"Hang in there. We'll figure out what's going on. See you tomorrow." He hung up the phone before Will had a chance to reply.

6

General Lee was sitting on a wooden chair, looking over maps. Dan studied him for a moment, instinctively knowing he was not to speak until spoken to. Immaculately dressed in his uniform, complete with a white shirt, black bow tie, and a gray vest, Dan knew the general's boots would be highly polished as well. Three gold stars were centered on each lapel of his jacket. His hair and beard were neatly trimmed. Dan was in total awe of this legendary figure. When Lee finally looked up, there was no hatred in his eyes.

7

The fifty-six year old Confederate general stood up and stared at the visitor through incredibly blue eyes, certain that this man had seen combat. He marveled at the green uniform, and the boots. Though a few inches taller, the man kept his gaze straight ahead, not looking down into his eyes. The Negro man had outstanding military bearing. He finally spoke.

"The two men who brought you into my camp told my guard that you are a brigadier general in the Union Army?"

"Yes, sir, but I have been retired for several years."

Lee stared at the black man standing in front of him. He didn't appear old enough to be retired and why would he be retired with a war going on? "What exactly do you mean, General?" he inquired with disbelief in his voice.

"Rodin, sir. Daniel Rodin. My story might take some time to explain. Would you mind terribly if I sat and could I please have a drink of water?"

Lee nodded as they both sat down. He summoned the guard to bring them a pitcher of water and two cups.

After Dan had a long drink of water, he asked, "General, would you mind if I smoke? I know you do not use tobacco, but unfortunately, smoking is one of my all too many vices."

Lee nodded again and Dan pulled a pack of cigarettes from his breast pocket. He lit one with a Zippo lighter. Dan handed him the pack and the lighter to study while he smoked.

He took a cigarette from the pack and marveled at how perfectly shaped it was, but he was confused by the filter. "What is this on the end of the cigarette and how did you make the cigarette so perfect? I do not smoke, it is true, but I have seen many homemade cigarettes; however, none the quality of the ones in this package."

After Lee put the cigarette back in the pack and picked up the lighter, Dan replied, "Sir, where I come from, everyone smokes cigarettes as well made as these. The brown part is called a filter. It is there to make the smoke less pungent and to take out some of the toxic chemicals from the tobacco. The lighter in your hand is a very simple tool to use. You simply spin the wheel, which strikes the flint and sets off a spark, lighting the wick. The container is filled with a flammable fluid and I can light hundreds of cigarettes before having to add any more fluid."

He was stunned. "Are these manufactured in the North?" He flicked the lighter on and off several times, marveling at it and smiling.

"Yes, sir. They are made in Bradford, Pennsylvania." He paused for a moment until he had Lee's attention. "The company was founded in nineteen thirty two." He paused again. "Sir, I was a brigadier general in the United States Army, but not the army you and your men are now fighting. Somehow I fell into a time warp and arrived here in eighteen sixty-three. The time I live in now is two thousand and thirteen."

Lee jumped to his feet. "Sir, that is not possible. How can a man from the future come back in time?"

Dan shrugged his shoulders. "General, I wish I knew how to explain my presence here for you to understand, but I don't even understand what happened." He took a deep drag from his cigarette. "Earlier today, I set up camp on the other side of a ridge to the south of your camp as a storm approached. I called a friend of mine on my cell phone and he said he didn't see..."

"You called him from your cell phone? What in blazes is that?"

He pulled his phone from his pocket and explained how it worked. "I can even take a photograph of you, sir. Do I have your permission?"

"You may."

Dan clicked the picture and handed him the phone.

He was completely flabbergasted, trying to assimilate the few things he had already learned.

"Sir, I know my story is hard to believe, but how would you explain the things I have already shared with you unless I am truly from the future?"

8

Lee pondered the question for several moments, and then shrugged his shoulders. "General Rodin, I certainly cannot explain, nor understand, the things you have been telling me, but one fact still remains: you are a general officer in the Army of the United States. Thereby, you will be treated as a prisoner of war, no matter that you are a colored man. I will make arrangements for you to be treated with respect in accordance with your rank, but let me assure you, sir, we will talk again at great length. If your story is true, it would be quite obvious that you know the outcome of this war; an outcome that I fear. You may also possess the information I will need to have to defeat the Union Army and win this war, after all. Please empty your pockets and place the contents on my desk." He stood up and summoned the guard, who quickly entered and stood at attention.

"Corporal, take the prisoner to an empty tent and do not let him out of your sight for one moment. I will send someone to relieve you in two hours. General Rodin is not to be bound in any manner, nor will anyone in his presence degrade him in any way because of the color of his skin. Do I make myself clear?"

"Yes, sir. I will take good care of the prisoner."

General Lee nodded his head. "Dismissed.

He sat down and wondered if he issued the right order to the corporal. He was not racist in any way, but he had to follow the policies of his government; a government that embraced slavery. However, Rodin was a general officer according to the card he showed him. He was so astonished with everything Rodin showed him, and he was beginning to believe that time travel was indeed possible.

9

As Dan was escorted from the tent, he looked back over his shoulder to see Robert E. Lee pick up his journal and Haskins' book. His hopes for a quick escape were no longer possible, but somehow, he would get away.

Soldiers who'd heard about the nigger general had gathered to stare at him; the hatred in most of their eyes was apparent, yet he had to smile; the military communication system, word of mouth, worked marvelously even during this age. A soldier's curiosity always had to be satisfied.

10

A photographer, resplendent in a black suit and a stovepipe hat, planted a tripod in the ground; hurriedly he mounted his wooden box camera, and rushed to intercept Dan and the soldier escorting him to his detention tent. "Excuse me, Corporal, but I would like to take a photograph of you and the prisoner. If you both would please step over here." He pointed to a spot just to the left of a tent. "I do believe I still have enough light to capture your images."

The corporal gently placed a hand on Dan's shoulder and guided him to the place the photographer pointed out.

They both stood very still while the man peered at them through a hole in the top of the camera box. He adjusted the tripod for their height, repositioned the camera angle, and then slipped a wet glass plate into the back of the camera. "Now, don't move. I need fifteen to thirty seconds of exposure to make sure your images are imprinted on the plate."

Dan was amused, but also troubled that the photographer had documented his visit to the past. How would this affect history? If I manage to get back to my own time, will I come back to a different world? Will the Confederacy have won the war and the United States broken in half? Would all the other following wars have occurred? Somehow I have to make sure that the Union army is not defeated at Gettysburg.

The photographer concluded his work and Dan was escorted to an empty tent. "You make yourself at home in there, General. I'll see to it that nobody bothers you."

Once inside, with the tent flaps closed, he sat down to think.

11

Robert E Lee poured another glass of water as he continued reading Haskins' book. He was up to the chapter that put the Confederate Army at this very place on this very day. Lee finished the page, turned to the next, and found a blank page. As he thumbed through the rest of the book, he found all the pages blank. After considerable thought, he decided that since this was a book of history, possibly transported to the past by some quirk of nature, nothing more would appear until events unfolded in this time. He was certainly going to run his theory past Rodin.

He picked up Rodin's personal journal and read entries he could not even begin to understand, so he put it away. Next he picked up the cell phone and was baffled by the numbers, words and symbols. Though all of this was beyond his comprehension, he knew full well that if all this came from the future, communication in the future must be truly amazing, but being able to call anyone in the world and having them speak to you in seconds was totally beyond his intellectual capacity. He put the phone down and then looked through the binoculars. They were far superior to the ones he used on the battlefield. He summoned his guard. "Private, would you please find Corporal Haskins and bring him to my tent."

"Yes, sir." Private Lenke left the tent, knowing where he would find Haskins in short order.

After Haskins reported and saluted, Lee returned the salute and put the corporal at ease. "Corporal, did you see that General Rodin was situated in his tent and placed under guard?"

"Yes, sir. I was guarding him myself since I escorted him to his tent."

"Have you been keeping a journal?"

"Yes, sir. I have been keeping a journal for the past few weeks."

"Corporal, did you tell General Rodin your name?"

"No, sir. May I ask why you want to know? I didn't think I would be giving away any information by telling him my name if I was asked?"

"Son, take a seat. What I am about to show you cannot be told to anyone in this camp. Is that understood?"

"Yes, sir." He stated, apprehensively.

He slid the book across his desk and Haskins picked it up. He looked at the title on the cover, saw his name, and opened the book to the first page. His mouth flew open when he saw the publication date was 1871.

12

Dan sat on the grass inside his tent. He lit up a cigarette; his smokes and the lighter being the only two things he was allowed to have during his incarceration. He had been in quite a few life threatening and life changing situations during his military career, but nothing compared to this. Trapped in the past, with no idea of how long it would last was an overwhelming feeling, not to mention the worst-case scenario that he might never return and die here before he was even born.

Bone tired, he fell asleep and he relived the horror of that day near Xuan Loc.

****

The platoon had been patrolling for several days, coming into contact seven times with small bands of Viet Cong. Due to this heavy activity; he radioed headquarters that they might be nearing a VC stronghold.

After he got off the horn with the old man, he walked over to sit with Will and his brother, Harry. They looked up as he approached. Despite being a friend and a brother, he was also their commanding officer, and they gave him due respect for his rank.

"Hey, LT, what's going on?" Harry smiled at his brother.

Dan sat down on the hard packed ground and lit a cigarette. "I just called Captain Lowell and told him about what's been going down the past few days and that we suspected we might be nearing a VC stronghold. The old man told me to hang tight right here and he would send in another platoon before we continued on. I have a bad feeling we're going to get in some really nasty shit before this is all over." He looked at them, waiting for their comments, comments he valued highly.

Will continued whittling a stick with the brand new pocketknife his folks sent to him in the mail. "You know, LT, you may be right. The hairs on the back of my neck have been standing up almost all morning. I think we're close, and the VC will not press an attack until they get us in a kill zone. They probably figured you'd call the company for more men. It's going to be a turkey shoot for them." He looked up into his friend's eyes. "Dan, I don't want to die in the godforsaken place."

He nodded and then looked at his brother.

Harry pursed his lips. "I think Will is right. A lot of us will be going home in bags in the next day or so, and I don't want that to happen to anyone, especially the three of us. We have too much to do with our lives to have them end here in Vietnam. Plus, we are getting much too short for this shit." A wry smile crossed his face. The three of them had come to 'Nam together and had less than thirty days to go before heading home. They knew about the rule that two brothers could not serve in combat at the same time unless they volunteered. They volunteered to go together and Will was not going to let them go without him.

Dan closed his eyes for a moment and thought about home, their parents and friends. He watched

Will whittle, admiring the knife in his hands. "When did you get that knife? Can I see it?"

After closing the blade inside, he flipped it to him. Dan opened it, tested the edge of the blade with his hand and whistled. "Sucker's really sharp." After closing it, he threw it back.

"Yeah, I just got it a couple of days ago from my dad, and he put a hell of an edge on it before he mailed it."

Harry pulled back the charging handle of his weapon and checked the chamber. "Guess we're going to really get into some heavy shit soon."

Dan rubbed sweat from his eyes with his dirty hands and nodded "'Fraid so, brother. Headquarters probably sees this clusterfuck as a chance to catch the enemy where they live, but I'm sure with our under strength platoon and even with fifty more warm bodies, I think we are going to be outgunned at least three to one, plus the gooks are going to be dug in pretty good. Cobras will get some, but there's going to be plenty of gooks for us to kill, or," he paused, "to kill us."

Moments later he heard the sound of multiple rotors about five minutes out from the platoon's position. He stood up, looked at his friends and said, "Time to go earn our pay, guys." They followed him to the LZ to hook up with the rest of the men.

After the slicks landed, three Cobra gunships took off toward the suspected VC stronghold. The 84 men now walking toward the jungle could hear the sounds of miniguns, rockets and AK-47 fire in the distance.

Fifteen minutes later, after the Cobras softened up the area, the men spread out on line. Dan stumbled across a couple of dead dinks amidst trees torn and ripped apart by gunfire and rockets.

He scanned the woods, assuming VC soldiers would be well concealed inside camouflaged bunkers and tied to the upper branches of trees, watching them approach. When the firefight began, he and his men saw muzzle flashes, but no targets to shoot back at. Several soldiers died in the first burst before the rest of the platoon could get to cover. The gun ships returned and laid down a heavy volume of fire from above the treetops, killing some more of them, but it wasn't enough. As Dan fired his M-16, he saw a half dozen gooks pop up from spider holes on his left flank. They charged toward Will and Harry. Dan stood up and killed all six of the enemy before they could harm his friend and his brother. He moved closer to the bunkers, tossed grenades and sprayed the communists with his M-16. More men charged the enemy positions and killed many of the slant eyed bastards, but three more Americans died. He then took out the machine gun emplacement with rifle fire and a well-placed grenade.

About a half hour later, the remaining enemy soldiers disappeared into tunnels, spider holes, and the thick jungle. The fight was over. American losses were twenty-four dead, seventeen wounded, and one missing.

The platoon swept the area and counted one hundred and seventeen dead gooks. Eighty-three enemy weapons were found and stacked for destruction.

Dan sat on a log and lit a cigarette. Harry and Will came over to join him.

"Damn, LT. You were like a maniac out there, but if you hadn't charged those bunkers, and got those other guys to follow you, a lot more of us would probably be in body bags now." Will took out his pocketknife, etched LTDAN in the handle with another knife and gave it to his friend. "Hey buddy, this is yours now. You earned it for saving my bacon today."

Dan grinned and accepted the gift. "This will never leave my person, not ever!"

****

He awakened, startled, as nightmares usually awakened him. This was the first time in all these years his knife was not with him. He dropped it on the ground near his campfire after he heard the musket fire and he never gave it a thought until now. If Will came looking for him, he might find it. Since the knife was in the campsite, it might signal that he was in trouble, but he knew that expecting anyone to imagine he was trapped in the past was asking too much. Discouraged, he lay down to try to get some sleep. He would need to save his strength in case he got an opportunity to escape. Escape to where? He was very concerned about Haskins' journal. The book really covered the Battle of Gettysburg and Lee would certainly figure out a way to use it to his advantage; changing his tactics, especially to get to the high ground, or even perhaps to send his army around Gettysburg and hit the Union army in the rear, away from the devastating cannon fire they would have to face with frontal attacks. As these thoughts ran through his mind, he drifted off to sleep again.

13

Haskins read his words as General Lee watched him. After he read about yesterday's events, he turned the page and saw it was blank, as was every other page afterward. The corporal looked up at his general. "Marse Robert, I don't understand this? Why is the rest of the book filled with blank pages? Would a publisher include blank pages?" He began to shake, uncontrollably.

Lee got up from his desk and came around to comfort the boy. "I don't know son, but the only thing I can figure is that since you haven't written the next entry, the book, as General Rodin described to me, will not show anything until you write again."

Haskins accepted this from his commander with a nod. "General, do you think if I make an entry in my journal tonight, the words will appear in the book?"

Lee considered this for a moment, and then smiled. "Go do some writing, son, and let's see what happens. However, I don't think you should write anything about what we have discussed here, nor should you write anything about General Rodin. Write as though it is just another day in the army."

Am I afraid that if he writes about Rodin, there would be no way to change history? We must defeat the Union at all costs. When Haskins departed, Lee felt the need to rest so he lay down on his cot and closed his eyes.

14

Will pulled into the Amoco station in Elkridge to gas up and get a cup of coffee. He needed caffeine to keep him awake for a couple more hours to do some research on his computer. He wanted to try to find the guys from the platoon to see if they were experiencing any unusual feelings or memories. He also wanted to have a conversation with Dr. Nelson Wainwright. He met the scientist at one of his speaking engagements two years ago and they had become friends. He was considered a wacko in a lot of circles with his theories about time travel. Though he was a time travel buff as well, Wainwright's website amused him on previous visits, but now he needed to try to get some answers-maybe even find out if he could somehow be sent back to the past, find Dan, and bring him back to the present.

Two hours of searching veteran websites finally led him to two guys from the platoon. After phoning them, exchanging pleasantries and addresses, he asked them several questions, but everything seemed normal with them. He came to the conclusion that perhaps nothing would change if Dan had been transported to the past. However, if he had time traveled to the Civil War, the Confederates might get information from him that could lead to a Union defeat. If that happened, he and many others might not even exist in the present day, and the whole future of mankind could be changed. He began rubbing his temples to temporarily ward off the headache that was becoming a mild, but persistent, throb. It was time to walk away from the computer; he needed to talk to Nelson, even though it was after eleven. He held the knife in his hands, trying to judge how long it could have been there. Plus reviewing Dan's previous hunts, knowing he had never been to that place before. Is it really possible that Dan could have traveled through time? He had just placed his hand the phone as it started to ring; startled, he picked it up and said a quick. "Hello?"

"Will, Nelson Wainwright here. How are you, my friend?"

He was shocked. "Nelson! I was just about to dial your number. This is quite a coincidence."

"Perhaps, but you may not think so after you hear why I called."

He waited a long moment for his friend to speak.

"Will, I know where Dan is, and I figured you would be calling me sometime tonight. After I talked to my people and called Harry, this is the first opportunity I had to phone you."

"I don't understand. How can you know where he is? I came to the conclusion that he had somehow been transported to the past, but how could you know that, unless your research into time travel has been much more than research."

"There is a lot you now need to know. I want you to come to Washington immediately. Harry will be here in a few hours. Come to the Vietnam Memorial and I'll meet you there at six tomorrow morning. Will, time travel is not only possible; it has been a reality for six years. There's too much to tell you in a phone conversation, but when we meet, I'll answer all your questions." He hung up.

He held the phone for a long time, listening to the dial tone, before he placed it back in the cradle. Time travel is not only possible; it has been a reality for six years! The sentence kept running through his head as he packed a bag. He kissed his sleepy wife goodbye and told her he had to go to Washington, but he didn't tell her why, or how long he would be gone. She trusted him implicitly, knowing he would explain everything when he could or was allowed to do so. She turned on her side and went back to sleep.

Will Jennings and Harry Rodin were both on their way to the nation's capital to learn more about the government's time travel program.

15

Most of the soldiers in camp were asleep, but Dan was having trouble getting comfortable. Although he had slept in much worse places during his tour of duty in Vietnam, his discomfort was more mental than physical. Here he was in 1863, in a Confederate camp, a little more than three full days before the battle of Gettysburg would commence. He rolled over on his side and closed his eyes. Moments later, he heard someone come into the tent and he opened his eyes and sat up. General Lee stood there holding a lantern.

"General Rodin, I assume that where you come from this is not the most comfortable place you have ever tried to sleep, but I'm afraid it is the best I could do for you."

Rodin smiled. "General Lee, I've slept in much worse places in my army career. As combat veterans, we both know that comfort is not usually found on the battlefield."

Lee set the lantern down and a soldier brought in a stool. After the soldier was dismissed, he took a seat and handed him Haskins' book. "Take a look through that book, sir, and tell me what you make of it."

He began paging through until he came to the first blank page, and then he paged through the rest of the blank book. He shook his head, perplexed. "I know when I purchased this book, all the pages were filled with events of this war. I can only guess that since

Haskins hasn't written anything more, the book can't be complete." He scratched his head. "I admit I am as mystified as you are, sir. I still don't know how I could have traveled through time without a device to send me here or get me back to my own time. In my time, exploring the past and the future has been studied, but nobody has ever come up with a way to make it possible, yet here I am in 1863."

Though he still did not fully believe Rodin was from the future, or that the north had won, he inquired, "What do you think will happen if the Confederacy wins this war?"

Dan sighed, lit up a cigarette and smoked thoughtfully for a few moments. "Robert, I have to be totally honest. I don't know what my presence here, or the Confederacy winning the war, would do to upset the balance of future events, but I can imagine the results would be catastrophic."

Lee seemed nonplussed by the use of his Christian name. "Daniel, I wish I knew as well. I certainly want to win the war because I am a Virginian, but since meeting you, I am having reservations about what this country would be like broken in half. I am going to have to go back to my tent and ponder this thought for a long time before I make a decision..."

"General," he interrupted, "Look at it this way. If you decide to change history, the men destined to die may live and the men that should live may die. The descendants of the men who died will never be born and those lost souls may have been destined to perform great feats that may benefit all mankind. Then imagine a worst-case scenario. The ancestors of the men who lived and should have died may be perpetrators of evil. Are you prepared to tamper with destiny and make Divine decisions?"

After several moments of thought, he replied, "Yes, I understand what you are saying, but what if your theories create no effect on the future. I could be throwing away a glorious opportunity to install the Confederate States of America as a great power to be reckoned with by the rest of the world." He leaned forward, waiting for a response.

Dan did not know what to say. How could he make him understand that he was so afraid of what might happen to his life in the future. "General, I am just one man, a man from the future, it is true, but I beg you to stay with the course of action that is about to happen. Chances are, my presence here alone may alter impending events, but if you find a way to win the war, I think time could be reformed in devastating ways. I fear if the United States is broken in two, imminent world powers will have a much easier time of drawing us into war and defeating us. Obviously, I am trying to influence your decision, but I know that you are an honorable man and whatever I say will not sway you from what you decide to do."

Lee stood up. "I will give this much thought and we will speak again in the morning. Try to get some rest, sir." He turned and walked out of the tent, leaving the journal. He turned and pleaded, "Please do not open the journal until we meet again in the morning."

Dan lay awake for a long time before sleep finally won out, but it was not a restful sleep. The journal of Andrew Haskins lay, unopened, beside him on the grass.

June 28th

1

At five-thirty, just as Will was walking to the Vietnam Memorial in 2012, Dan was awakening in 1863. He rubbed the sleep from his eyes and pulled his knees toward his chin to loosen up his back. He slept fitfully at best, dreams of Vietnam and the Battle of Gettysburg churning through his mind. He rotated his neck a few times and then sat up, looking at the journal lying on the grass. Tempted to open it, he stuffed the journal inside his shirt just before a guard came in to escort him to breakfast.

When they stepped outside the tent, Dan saw most of the men in camp were awake. Some were still eating breakfast while others were cleaning weapons, probably preparing to go on patrol. He knew that Lee would be camped here until the morning of the 30th. He recalled reading this in a book about the invasion in 1863. The general held his councils of war here since the 26th, and it was here at Shetter's Woods that he planned and ordered an attack on Harrisburg. On the 29th, he received information from General Longstreet of the whereabouts of the Army of the Potomac and it was then that he decided to cross South Mountain and meet the Yankees at a place on a direct line toward Baltimore and Washington, D.C. That place was Gettysburg. Three more full days until the battle was to begin and he still had no clue how to escape and warn the Union Army, nor how to convince Robert E. Lee not to change history.

After his meal, a Johnnie Cake, which was basically a cornmeal biscuit, and a cup of very strong coffee, he lit up a cigarette, offering one to his guard, who gratefully accepted, though he was leery about the filter.

The guard inhaled, held the smoke in and then expelled it from his nose and mouth. "Say, General, this is a mighty fine smoke, but what is this thing on the end of it?"

Rodin thought for a moment, wondering what he should tell the soldier. Since Lee ordered him not to tell anyone he was from the future, he said, "It's called a filter. It was invented in the North, but people didn't like them, so the inventor stopped making them, plus putting the filters on cost far too much money. I guess I bought the last of them a few months ago."

"How much did you have to pay for these cigarettes?"

"They were very dear. Cost me almost six dollars for twenty. I only have about four left, so I guess I'll have to go back to rolling my own." He smiled then chuckled. The soldier smiled back.

"I guess I'll be heading out on patrol soon. I sure am itching to get into a fight with some Yankees. I been in the army 'bout three months now and haven't seen any real combat, jest a few little skirmishes."

Dan glared at him and replied in a venomous tone, "I imagine you Rebs will get all the fighting you want until this war is over." He calmed back down and then inquired, "Are they going to send me to a POW camp?"

He raised his eyebrows and then took another drag. "I don't rightly know, General, but I think you'll be coming with us until General Lee figures out what to do with you. Where do you call home?"

"I was born in Virginia, but we moved to Ohio when I was just a little tyke." As he thought about those times, a sergeant approached.

"General Rodin. General Lee wishes to speak to you immediately." His voice dripped with sarcasm as he offered the black man a mock salute.

The guard escorted Dan inside, saluted his beloved commander, turned and walked outside.

Rodin was offered a seat. "Daniel, did you sleep well?" Lee inquired as he shuffled through some papers on his table.

Dan shook his head. "No, Robert, I had a horrible night. In my army career I have slept in many uncomfortable places, but I think the fact of being in 1863 made the discomfort even worse."

Lee sat down and poured two cups of coffee, handing his guest one. "Did you bring Haskins' book with you?"

"Yes, sir. I did."

"Have you opened it this morning?"

"No, sir. I have not."

"May I see it, please?"

"Of course." He extracted it from a fatigue pocket and handed it to Lee.

The general flipped through the pages until he came to the last page he had read last evening. He turned the page and smiled, handing it back.

Dan's curiosity was aroused as he also looked at the page, which had been blank the night before. It was now filled with an entry that Haskins must have written before retiring last night. This proved his theory that history, as he knew it, unfolded as Haskins wrote in his journal. Dan's presence in the past may have already changed things if Haskins wrote something different now. What more would change if Lee forced him to reveal the Union's positions at Gettysburg? A chill ran down his spine. He had no clue how he was going to stop the Confederates from winning this battle, and perhaps even the war.

He looked into Lee's eyes. "General. I implore you not to change the course of history. It could have severe repercussions on what will happen from this day forward. The United States and the Confederate States could be wiped off the map by future superpowers. Can you even picture a future without America?"

Lee thoughtfully sipped his coffee, then said, "You have posed an interesting question, General, but if the Confederacy wins, perhaps none of the future wars will ever occur. Is that possible?"

Now it was Rodin's turn to think. After a minute or so, he replied, "That certainly is possible, Robert, but I shudder to think how bad it would be for future Americans from both the North and the South if war does indeed occur and we are not united as one nation. Just look at how difficult it is for your army. The South does not have the industrial capability of the North and you must seek other ways to get your weapons and munitions, not to mention food and other goods. The United States as a whole is so vastly rich in resources that as one nation, we can produce nearly everything we need to be the major power of the world. General, I wish I could take you back to my time to show you how great the United States is.

Granted, we still have our problems, but I would not want to live anywhere else on the face of the earth."

The tent flap opened and a sergeant said, "Sir, I am sorry to interrupt, but a courier has just arrived and he needs to speak to you immediately."

Lee stood. "Very well, Sergeant. Please have him step in." The sergeant saluted. Lee nodded. "Dismissed." After the sergeant left the tent, Lee said to Rodin, "I will have to give this much more thought before I make a decision."

The two generals stepped outside. Lee looked around and saw two soldiers with seemingly nothing to do. They saw him looking their way and he shouted, "You two soldiers, come here."

They scrambled up to their commanding officer and saluted.

"I want you both to guard General Rodin and show him the courtesy an officer should receive." He ordered.

One of the soldiers replied, "But, sir, he's a nigger."

Lee closed his eyes and when he opened them; his eyes were filled with fury. "Yes, this man is a Negro, but he is a general officer of the Union army and you will treat him well. Is that understood?"

Both men nodded although they still gave Rodin dirty looks as they escorted him to a copse of trees away from the campfire.

2

Will stood by the Three Soldiers statue at the Vietnam Memorial. He hadn't seen it since the tenth anniversary of The Wall in 1992. The bronze statue was a grouping of three young men, dressed in Vietnam jungle fatigues, and carrying weapons of that time. They represented Caucasian, African American, and Hispanic soldiers. He turned his gaze to the enormity of the Vietnam Memorial, etched with over 58,000 names, approximately seven thousand more than the number of casualties at the Battle of Gettysburg.

Harry came up beside him. "It's quite impressive, isn't it?"

Will smiled at his friend and shook his hand. "Yeah, it is. Ya know if it wasn't for Dan, our names would probably be etched here, too."

He nodded. "I thought I'd never be able to repay my brother for saving my life, but now...who knows? I guess Nelson will be here soon to tell us what he has in mind. I still can't believe time travel has been a reality for six years."

"Yeah, me neither. I sure am anxious to see how it works. I have a gut feeling that we're gonna find ourselves back in 1863 in the very near future."

Harry nodded in agreement just as Nelson joined them.

Nelson shook Harry's hand. "It is a pleasure to meet you. Will has spoken often of you and Dan and I feel I already know you pretty well."

"The pleasure is mine. I've been interested in time travel for a long time and you have certainly written several interesting books."

"Thanks." He looked at the expanse of black granite and then walked toward it.

They walked the path along The Wall, passing groups of veterans, even at this early hour. Many took rubbings, saluted the black granite, and left gifts at its base.

"I know you guys have a lot of questions and they will be answered as soon as we reach the Time Travel Facility. We simply call it the TTF As far as we know, Dan is safe, but the problem we have is that General Lee might try to change the course of the war, which could lead to a Confederate victory and the timeline of world history could change dramatically. We have some theories of what could happen to the world if that occurs and I have printouts for both of you to read while we are driving. You won't be able to see outside once in the vehicle because, even though you are going to the TTF, I cannot allow you to see where it is for security purposes. Hold all your questions until we are in the limo." Nelson quickened his pace to be a few steps in front of his friends.

They were stunned and looked at each other, but they said nothing until they were seated inside the limousine.

Harry spoke first. "Nelson, how do you know Dan is safe?"

As he handed them the printouts he answered, "When we realized that he was thrown into the past, we immediately sent two soldiers, Time Travel Inspectors, TTIs for short, back to find him and to see if anything perceptible had changed pursuant to him being there. They reported in a few hours ago and told us that he was inside Lee's tent. They told us that Dan told Lee he is from the future. He saw Dan's cell phone, lighter, binoculars, a journal, and a pack of cigarettes, but the one thing that really is disturbing is that he saw a book written by one of his soldiers. He might read the book and figure out what he would have to do to defeat the Union army at Gettysburg and possibly win the war."

Will asked, "If you have two men back there, why haven't they just pulled Dan out and brought him back to today?" *How did they report in?*

"Both good questions, my friend, but you have to wait until you are inside the facility for answers. I know you have many more questions, but I urge you to take our remaining time on the road to read those printouts so you will know what could happen to all of us as more changes occur."

They knew they would get nothing more from him, so they continued reading, both of them stunned by the theories presented.

After the Confederacy won the war in 1864, capturing Washington, D.C., Abraham Lincoln was removed from office, tried and hanged. Jefferson Davis moved his office and staff to Washington, appointing General Lee as Vice-President. Lee would keep an office in Richmond and the two leaders would be in constant contact via telegraph. The Confederate States of America would not enter World War I and all of Europe would fall to the German war machine. World War II would last fifteen years before Germany and Japan were defeated, at horrendous cost in men and material. The Korean War never happened, but the Vietnam War, lasting twenty two years, practically bankrupted the nation. By 1990, the government had collapsed; Eighty percent of the population was without work and the USSR invaded our shores. The Hammer and Sickle replaced the Stars and Bars as the flag of this once great nation and we have been under Communist rule since that time.

When they finished reading, they looked at each other and then they looked at Nelson, who just shrugged his shoulders.

The three men knew that they had to do whatever it would take to keep history on track; the consequences could be far worse than even the theories that had been proposed by some of the most brilliant men on the planet.

3

Sergeant Behr ordered Dan to sit down at the base of a tree about a hundred feet from the center of camp, then positioned himself to utilize his peripheral vision, keeping both the prisoner and the camp in view. Dan had passed this tree when the two Rebs brought him into the camp. He became concerned about his tent and rucksack that were on the other side of the ridge. If they were found more questions would be raised. He would never know that before the two soldiers, Luke and Billy Joe saw him, the tent and rucksack disappeared.

The other guard sat down next to Dan. "General Rodin, I am sorry I had to lash out at you like that. I'm Staff Sergeant Kenneth Younes and my friend is Sergeant Arlen Behr. We've been sent here from 2013 to keep watch over you."

Dan's eyes widened momentarily. "You have been sent here? Time travel has been perfected? How?"

Younes brought his finger to his lips. "General, please keep your voice down. This charade has to last as long as we're here. It is a long story and Arlen or I hope to have the time to fill you in on everything. I know for a fact that sometime today or tomorrow your brother and Will Jennings will be joining us. Our mission is to make sure that the Confederates do not win at Gettysburg."

Dan looked at the ground. "I know, Sergeant. I figured if major changes occur, there would be a ripple effect that will alter the course of future events, and that could truly be disastrous. How are we going to ensure the future stays intact?"

"It's not gonna be easy, sir, especially since Lee knows you are from the future. That knowledge alone could alter every decision he makes. Somehow we have to keep him to the course he has already planned, and as long as the battle unfolds the way it should, the results might not cause too much damage to the future. The question is how do we accomplish that feat?"

Their attention was diverted by a group of Confederates that were little more than boys. Dan watched them stroll by. "It's a given, Ken, that the futures of some of those soldiers could definitely change because some of the men who would have lived, won't, and some who would have died will live."

Over his shoulder, Arlen said, "Ken, cool it. A couple of Rebs are coming this way."

When they approached, one said, "Howdy boys. How is the nigger general doing?"

Ken looked toward them and saw the Reb who had spoken was a middle-aged sergeant missing two teeth. He smiled. "Sergeant, this here nigger is doing just fine, but he don't talk much though. I guess being a nigger general gives him the right not to talk to enlisted scum like us."

The four men in Confederate uniforms laughed loudly as Dan just stared them down.

The sergeant walked over to Rodin and knelt down. "Some of my men have big plans for you. One of those plans includes a rope and a tree, if you catch my drift." As he spoke, spittle sprayed on Dan's face. The Confederate sergeant stood up, looked back at Ken and Arlen and said, "You two men take good care of the general so's he's in good shape for when we hang his nigger ass."

Arlen laughed. "Don't you worry, Sergeant. We aren't going to let anything happen to him before the lynching."

The two soldiers headed back to camp. When they were out of earshot, Ken said "Guess we have a new problem, General."

He swallowed bile rising in his throat. "You guys got any ideas to keep me from getting strung up?"

4

After reading all the information Nelson gave him, Will went back to reread about the advent of time travel.

Lawrence Delp, a retired CIA agent and an avid spelunker discovered a wormhole in 1987. While searching a cave in northern Virginia, he entered the wormhole and came out in the year 1933. For two days he wandered around town taking in the sights and talking to people. He took notes in his journal and then found his way back to the hole, returning to 1987.

He informed the CIA chief about his discovery. Leading scientists and mathematicians were briefed about the project, and after twenty years of intense research, they perfected the method to enable a time traveler to be sent to a specified location using precise latitude and longitude calculations. The past could be breached but travel into the future was still not possible, though exploration continues.

Will was having difficulty absorbing all the information. "Nelson, I guess I understand the basic concept the wormhole, but I'll have to see everything before I really get it."

Harry stopped reading. "I agree with Will. There is so much to learn about the project, and what I've learned so far is truly astounding."

Nelson smiled. "I know exactly how you feel. When I was brought into the project I was totally flabbergasted by the enormity of the research that had already been done and I think that once you see what has been accomplished you will have a much better understanding."

The car stopped and the three men stepped out inside a huge elevator that began a slow descent. Nelson gave them badges to wear before the door opened into a small area where a burly sergeant major sat behind a desk. He looked at their badges then made several keystrokes on his computer. A steel door opened to a large room filled with computers, and a massive wall unit displaying four different scenes at the same time.

They saw a street, filled with pedestrians and automobiles from many years ago. In the distance an unfinished skyscraper rose high above the city, probably New York. Another scene depicted numerous sailboats on a lake. The third screen was ablaze with fire and firemen scurrying around to save several buildings and rescue their occupants. All the people in the TTF saw four people jump from the roof of one to their deaths on the street below. Images of people jumping from the Twin Towers in 2001 filled their minds. The fourth screen was the most intriguing. Dan Rodin was talking to two Confederate soldiers, one mature and balding and the other younger and blond. A technician minimized the other three views to allow the three men to focus solely on the Civil War view, complete with sound.

The balding man's words came through loud and clear. "General, I gotta admit it's gonna be a tough thing to stop because that sergeant sure wants to stretch your neck. The suits back at the TTF are surely listening in; probably your brother and Will too, and they'll find a way out for us."

Harry stared intently at the screen, trying to digest the fact that his brother had really been transported to 1863. The blond man turned away from Dan and the picture on the screen suddenly split in half. Dan and the older man remained on one side, but the on the other screen they watched Confederate soldiers going about their daily routines through the younger man's eyes. He shook his head. "I know we are seeing what your TIs see, but how did you accomplish that feat?"

"That, my friend remains a mystery to all of us. Somehow, when Time Inspectors are sent back, the energy that accompanies them to their destination allows us to see and hear exactly what they see and hear. When people are transported to another time period, even though they did not go back through this facility, we are able to see and hear what they are doing as well. That is how we knew Dan was in 1863. I wish I could offer more information, but I am as clueless as the top scientists who have been working on this project. I guess the creators of the sixties TV show, *The Time Tunnel*, weren't too far off with their impression about how time travel would work."

5

Dan frowned, picked up a rock, and threw it in frustration. "Ken, why can't you just take me back to 2013?"

"General, I hate to be the one to tell you this, but since you were transported back here by other means, I can't take you back though the wormhole. Our first attempt to bring someone back was a disaster. The man vaporized and we never tried it again. Our mission is to keep watch over people sent back by other means and make sure they don't alter the future in any way. I'm afraid you're trapped here, sir."

Dan's head drooped. Before meeting Ken and Arlen, he had no idea if he could ever make it back to his time, but when they introduced themselves his hopes soared; now his balloon was deflated again. He raised his head. "Men, that certainly doesn't bode well, but I was...no I still am, a soldier, and I have to look at this experience as a mission, possibly my most important ever!"

"Sir, I know the scientists will keep trying to come up with an answer, and if we can what we have to do here." Ken spoke softly, wanting to reach out and comfort him, but didn't, knowing that he was probably being watched.

6

As Harry and Will stared at the screen, Nelson gently laid his hands on their shoulders. "I'm sorry you had to find out this way, instead of getting an explanation from someone here in the facility, but we'll try to answer the questions you might have before you get sent back. Hopefully we'll find a way to bring him back safely. Small items have made the trip back here without any damage, but the time traveler vaporized. I know you're both concerned about those two Rebs, but I'm sure our soldiers will be able to keep them at bay."

Keeping his eyes on Dan, Harry said, "Somehow, we'll get my brother out of harm's way and keep history intact. When do we go?"

"We're going to insert you after dark, but before then, we need to get your papers ready and find the proper clothes." He led them to another part of the facility that was much like a commercial laundry, clothing suspended from a conveyer system. He keyed in some numbers on a PC and the garments moved toward them until several male and female articles were in reach. He picked two shirts and two pairs of trousers off the belt and turned the garments over to his friends. They were also given plastic bags filled with accessories.

The two men went into changing rooms and came out wearing mid 1800s clothing. Nelson was pleased with his selections, although they were scratching themselves, not comfortable with the way the coarse materials felt against their bodies. Will wore a burgundy work shirt, a pair of brown wool pants, sporting buttons at the waist for his black suspenders, a brown slouch hat with a wide brim, and brown boots. Harry had on a simple pair of black trousers, a little too short; held up by a piece of rope for a belt, and a red work shirt. He wore a pair of low cut shoes and no socks.

Harry pulled his shirttails from his trousers as he spoke. "How am I going to pull this off? When those Rebs see another black man, they might go ballistic."

"That's our next stop." They walked into an office where several men and women were seated at stations working on creating false documents. "Saundra is creating papers for both of you. Will, you're going to be a farmer from a nearby town who is a Confederate sympathizer and Harry is going to be a free man who works for you. You're going to leave from here on a wagon pulled by two mules. The wagon is being loaded with bags of wheat and baskets of vegetables that you're going to deliver to Lee's camp. Once you guys get there, you're pretty much on your own and you'll have to ad lib a way to stay in camp for a couple of days if possible."

Will chuckled. "You sure aren't gonna make our time travel experience easy, are you?"

"No I'm not. The things we are most concerned about is to keep the history timeline intact and getting Dan out of there as quickly as possible." His cell phone rang. "Yes. Okay, we will." He turned toward a 42 inch TV screen; Will and Harry did the same. The screen lit up showing Dan speaking to Ken. "Lee doesn't know what's going to happen because Haskins' book is incomplete. The events leading up to today are already written, but Lee has no clue as to what he needs to do to outmaneuver the Union defenses at Gettysburg. But he does know that he will be defeated and the Union will win the war."

7

Ken's gaze shifted toward Lee's tent in the distance and then he turned back to Dan "General, how much have you told him?"

"I didn't give him any particulars about the battle, but I fear that he will pay more attention to his staff and alter his battle plan and the historical course of the siege. That alone could cause massive repercussions. I don't see how we can keep him from doing that." When he told Ken about Haskins' book. Arlen was out of earshot, so he would have to be told later.

"I think there might be a way, General. Excuse me please." He walked behind a tree as if to urinate. He spoke to the people in the TTF. "The key is Haskins, I think. You guys have to find another copy of his book, so we can convince him to write exactly what has been already written, except instead of after the fact, he'll have to write events just before they occur. If that works, the battle should unfold properly."

8

"He may be right, guys. Give me a few minutes." Nelson walked to an elevator and went down one floor to a massive library.

Melanie and Stephanie, the two librarians looked up as he entered. "Ladies, I need you to locate a copy of this book. Hopefully we have one on hand, although I'm sure few copies exist." He handed Steph a slip of paper. She keyed the information into the computer and came up with a reference location. Mel stepped away from her desk and returned a few minutes later with a copy of Haskins' book. She handed it to him and sat back down at her desk.

"You two ladies are the best, you know." He saluted them and headed back upstairs.

Just then red lights began flashing and a siren blared out in three second bursts of sound. He ran back to the transport room with the other two men in hot pursuit.

Two techs were hurriedly tapping keystrokes on their PCs and a couple of soldiers stood by the huge hole in the rock that began to shimmer, conveying the appearance of green water cascading over the opening. In a moment a man, wearing the gray uniform of a Confederate soldier clutching his chest, spilled through the hole. He landed on his face, writhing in agony. Two soldiers picked him up and laid him on a gurney as a doctor and two nurses began working on him even as the he was being wheeled from the room.

The man was taken to an emergency room where doctors furiously worked on him. After an hour of surgery, he was stable; the mini ball removed from his chest had missed his heart by two inches. He had lost quite a bit of blood, but a transfusion would bring him back up to strength in short order.

When the doctor came out of the emergency room, Nelson was by his side. "Is he going to make it, doc?"

The doctor took off his gloves at the wash station and began to scrub. "He'll live, but he'll be out of it for a couple of hours. After he awakens, you will certainly have an opportunity to speak with him."

"Did he say anything before you put him under?"

The doctor looked up, his face furrowed. "Yes, he moaned and said, 'Damn Yankee shot me. Am I going to die?'" The doctor finished scrubbing and informed Nelson that his team found some identification in his uniform and the techs were working on that information to find out where he came from and when and where he was shot. "That's all I can tell you. Perhaps they've come up with something by now. The soldier's eyes were filled with fear, not only because of being shot, but he saw all the equipment in the operating room. I imagine he'll have a great many questions for you to answer, as well." He toweled off and strode away, exhausted.

Nelson raced back to the computer stations to see what they found out. When he arrived on the scene, Will and Harry were watching the screen, where Ken was still talking with Dan. Nelson spoke with some of the techs and after their conversation ended, he announced, "Guys, the man who stumbled through the portal is Private Benjamin Teague. He was shot on June 28th, 1863 just outside of where this facility now stands. He was reported missing and never returned home.

9

Later that morning, after receiving information from a courier regarding the whereabouts of the Army of the Potomac, Robert E. Lee, along with several bodyguards, took a ride to see General Longstreet. As he passed through the camp, cheers rose from the men lined up between the tents. He acknowledged their adoration for him with waves, doffs of his hat, and salutes. Though his men were exhausted from the long marches and previous battles, they were well fed. They scavenged vegetables from nearby farms, and had an abundance of protein from cattle and pigs. If they could get a little rest before the next battle, they might be able to drive the Yankees away, and then they could move toward Washington, DC.

Now, in the open countryside, he took in the features of the land, always looking for good ground to defend in the event those people, as he referred to Union soldiers, came on the attack. He knew however, that he and his Army of Northern Virginia would be on the offense, not the defense. God, how he wanted this war to end with a decisive victory in Pennsylvania, and then he would swing south again and march on Washington. I have to win here, or it could be all over. How many more good men will have to be sacrificed to attain victory? I have lost so many already. Yet, if I make decisions that will change the course of the history already written in the future, will America be able to survive broken in two?

The morning air was still cool, refreshing, for this time of year, especially after several days of rain that left the roads muddy in spots. Over an inch of rain had fallen over the past few days, and he was sure it would continue at least through the day. As he continued the few miles to General Longstreet's camp, he was deep in thought. *I need to talk to Pete and get his advice. He has always been a good leader and a fine friend, and his opinions mean a great deal to me.*

As they crested a rise, he saw the camp on the east side of the Conococheague Creek. He studied the remains of several iron ore forges that Pete's men destroyed while setting up camp. How many more forges the North had, he didn't know, but he was sure that they could keep producing war materiel for a very long time to come. Their resources were so plentiful and the Confederacy had so little.

Numerous Confederate soldiers whistled and whooped when they saw their beloved commander riding into camp. The raucous noise brought General James 'Pete' Longstreet out from the farmhouse that was his headquarters and he smiled as he watched Marse Robert greet his soldiers with smiles, waves, and salutes. Lee guided Traveller to the farmhouse. He dismounted and when Pete saluted, he returned it and then shook hands with his friend. "General Longstreet, you have chosen a fine area to make camp, and your men have certainly been busy denying those people further use of those forges."

"Yes, sir. Those damn Yankees can get iron almost anytime they need it, but the more forges we destroy; the longer it will take the enemy to rebuild. Would you care to step inside for some refreshment after your long ride?"

Lee smiled. "Indeed, I would like something cold to drink. I also need to ask you some questions."

After they stepped inside, Pete offered Lee a comfortable seat and an aide brought them a pitcher of cool water and two glasses. Lee sipped his water and sat quietly for a few moments. He could see on Pete's face that he was wondering what the hell he was really here for.

Lee looked up at his friend. "Have you heard any news about the location of the Army of the Potomac?"

"Well, sir, scouts have ridden back here with news that the Yankees are in Frederick, Maryland preparing to move north. I figure they're going to head up toward Emmitsburg, possibly as early as tomorrow morning. Fifteen minutes ago I also received news that Meade has replaced Hooker as commander of the whole Union army."

Lee's eyebrows shot upward as he sipped his water. "That is news. I know George from the Mexican War and he is a good soldier. I don't know how he'll be as commander of the Union forces but I'm sure we'll meet on the field of battle sooner than later. My couriers brought back the news of the Northern army as well, and I agree that they will be heading up toward Emmitsburg. What do you think about moving our army southeast to meet them somewhere down there? Perhaps if we beat them there, we'll have a clear road to Washington."

Longstreet sipped water and listened to his commander with great intent and respect. "Sir, I honestly think we need to rest here for a little while. Our troops are exhausted from the long days of marching and if we go into battle tired, I don't think we'd have a chance of beating them. Plus we don't really know much about the ground in the Emmitsburg area. We'd need some time to have mapmakers go out there and do some sketching to find the best place to defend against a Yankee attack. We also need to know what ground they would defend. I think we should take a few days before we set out again. The men are getting some good food and time to get sore feet and backs looked after. I know my men need at least a couple more days before they are ready to go again."

Lee stood up, signifying that the brief meeting had ended. "I will consider everything you said. I agree that the men are exhausted, and that a few days rest would do us all good, but I have a feeling that if we wait, we're going to get into a real bloodbath; one that could mean the end of our army and our cause." As he put his riding gloves on, he added, "Pete, I want this war over with as soon as possible. We've lost thousands of good men; men who could have done so much after the war to rebuild and defend the Confederate States, and I don't want to lose thousands more."

Longstreet laid a hand on the shoulder of his friend. "General, I too want this to end, but as long as the North can keep throwing men and materials into this conflict, we are going to have a tough time beating them. We have to meet them on the field of battle and destroy them as quickly as possible."

When Lee stepped from the house onto the porch, he saw a soldier holding Traveller's reins. He gave the man a sharp look and then his features softened with a smile crossing his face as recognition set in. He stepped from the porch and stuck out his hand. "Ben Tolliver, my goodness, it must be going on five years since I saw you last."

Tolliver saluted his commander and then put out his hand as well. "General Lee, sir. I figured you were close by, but I didn't expect I'd meet up with you."

Longstreet watched the reunion with total fascination. A thirty-year old private and a Confederate general were hugging like they were family.

After their embrace, Lee turned toward Longstreet. "General Longstreet, Private Tolliver is the son of one of my best friends, Ambrose Tolliver." He turned back to Ben. "How is your father doing?"

He lowered his head and said, "Daddy was killed last month at Winchester."

Lee placed his hands on his friend's shoulder. "I'm sorry. This putrid war keeps taking good friends of mine. I didn't know, son."

He looked up with tears in his eyes. "It's all right, sir. I hoped I'd meet up with you some day so I could tell you what happened. Do you have a few moments to spare?"

Pete said, "General Lee my headquarters is at your disposal. Please take all the time you need."

They stepped inside and sat down. Tears flowed down Ben's cheeks as he spoke. "Daddy was in the artillery and his battery was in the best spot to defend, called Fort Milroy after daddy's commander. General Milroy felt he could hold out for weeks with the defenses he had established. He had no idea that he was facing an entire corps.

"When the battle really got going, Daddy's fort was getting a pounding, not only from the enemy's guns." He looked up at Lee, who nodded. "They were also getting it from guns that were captured and turned on them. The battle lasted several hours before Milroy decided to try to cut their way out through Harper's Ferry.

"Near dawn, skirmishers laid down fire on the head of his column and the entire division was broken up. Daddy was gut shot, but he managed to get out of there alive and he was brought home to Ma and me, but he only lasted a couple of days before he died. That's when I decided to join up and fight."

"After this war is over, I promise to visit you and your ma. Your daddy was a good soldier and we served together for a long time. I was sorry to see him fight on the Yankee side, but I'm sure he fought well for what he believed in. I do appreciate you telling me what happened and I will see to it that General Longstreet watches over you so your ma doesn't lose a husband and a son."

They shook hands and hugged, and then Lee stepped outside again while Ben took a few moments to dry his eyes.

He slowly rode out of camp, to the cheers of his men lining the road. I couldn't tell Pete that our army will clash with those people at Gettysburg, because he would want to know how I came to that conclusion. I need to find a way to get more information out of General Rodin and change the course of this war. The South must prevail, especially for young men like Ben Tolliver who would die with honor for our cause.

10

Back at Lee's camp, the two rebels intent on hanging Rodin were conspiring with several other men. The ringleader, Sergeant James Stewart, led the conversation. "I don't like having that nigger in our camp, and General Lee has no business treating him special. If we hang his black ass while he's gone, nobody's gonna tell him who did it, anyway, nobody I know."

Private Jonas Sutherland looked into the eyes of his squad leader. "Sergeant Stewart, I don't like niggers neither, but if he finds out we hung him, we'd be in grievous trouble for sure."

"Sutherland, like I said, who would tell the general what happened? You know that most all of us hate them. They stink, they're stupid, and they ain't worth shit unless they're working for some Massa on a plantation. So why the hell should we keep him alive to eat our food and maybe escape and get to Yankee lines and tell them where we are. I'm always ready for a good fight with them blue bellies, but on our terms, not on theirs. We gotta string his black ass up darn quick, General Lee won't be gone too long, I spect."

The six men sitting in a circle all nodded their heads causing Stewart to smile through his missing teeth. "Let's go get him, boys."

11

Arlen Behr watched the gathering from the distance and when they stood up he said, "Ken, I think those soldiers are heading this way to string Dan up." He saw one of them duck inside a tent and come out with a long length of rope, confirming his suspicions.

Dan watched the Confederates walk toward them as other soldiers made room, or simply looked the other way. The lynching party drew closer and larger as more men joined them.

Ken and Arlen stood their ground in front of Dan, raising their rifles and pointing them at the swelling crowd of rebs. The mob stopped when they saw rifles pointed at them, but Stewart took a few more steps and said, "Boys, you don't want to make yourselves targets, too, do ya? If you stop us from hanging this nigger, you'll both be dead before the day is over." After a few moments of silence, he stepped closer and reached out his hand to pull the rifle away from Arlen.

When Stewart grabbed the rifle and pulled, Behr could not stop his finger from squeezing the trigger; a bullet from the fine tooled musket struck him in the chest, killing him instantly.

Lee had just ridden into camp and heard the shot. He quickly rode to where the mob glared at Ken and Arlen; several of the angry Confederates began to move toward the guards again. General Lee saw what was going on and drew his pistol: he fired a shot into the air, Most of the soldiers in the mob turned toward the sound of the shot, and when they saw who had that fired the shot, they began to disperse, but Lee ordered them to stand their ground.

He dismounted and ordered a few soldiers to keep the mob under guard until he had everyone's name. He looked at the body of Sergeant Stewart and then said to Behr, "Soldier, I will have to talk to you about what happened here. You may well have prevented the murder of General Rodin, but you have killed a fellow soldier and that is a grievous crime that will have to be dealt with. Please go to my tent and wait outside."

12

As Behr walked toward the command tent, Lee turned to Dan. "I am so sorry for what happened here today but I am sure you are well aware that many of my troops don't like colored folks and to have one here in their camp, being treated respectfully doesn't set too well with many of them." Lee was more than concerned about Dan's welfare because he needed to keep him alive to obtain more information about the upcoming battle. "I will deal with those men, I assure you, but I have much to do and..."

"General Lee, excuse me for interrupting, but the shooting was an accident. That sergeant grabbed the rifle and when he pulled it, it fired," Ken said.

Lee listened carefully and then looked at Dan. "Is this soldier's recollection of the shooting correct?"

"Yes, sir. I saw the shooting and that is what happened. I don't think my guard meant to kill a fellow Confederate soldier. I do believe he was willing to give his own life to protect mine. That certainly should speak very highly of how he obeys orders."

Lee studied both men very carefully for a few moments. He saw in their eyes that they were probably telling the truth. "Very well, I will take your statements into consideration when I speak to that soldier. What is his name and yours for that matter?" He directed the question to Ken.

"Sir, I am Private Younes and he is Private Behr."

"Private Younes, thank you for explaining what happened." He nodded at the two men, then grabbed Traveller's reins and walked toward his tent.

13

Dan walked back to the shade of the tree he had been sitting at with Younes still doing a convincing job of being his guard, even to the point of Ken prodding him firmly with his rifle. He muttered under his breath, "Geez, is that really necessary? I think everyone believes that you are a Confederate soldier. By the way, what were you going to take from your pack when the mob got really unruly?"

"I noticed some of them really looking us over and I don't want them to get any ideas that I may not be doing my job as real soldiers of this time would. I'll give you a little warning the next time. I nearly pulled the Uzi out of my pack, but I brought it along in case I really needed some firepower to get us out of a situation. Obviously, the people back at the TTF now know I broke a rule by coming here with a future weapon, and I'll get an ass chewing when we get back, but I'm going to protect you, and us, with any means at my disposal."

Dan fidgeted some, and replied, "Trust me; I'm not unhappy that you brought a weapon with you. If it gets captured or you lose it, there could be dire consequences, but if we can't keep Lee on the right track, everything is going to go to hell in a handbasket anyway, so we don't have anything to lose, do we?"

"No, General, we don't. Hopefully when Will and Harry arrive, we'll be able to figure out a way to get you out of here, and let the chips fall as they may with the course of the war."

Dan shook his head slightly. "No. The primary mission is to keep Lee on track and my return to the future is secondary. Let's just wait this day out and tonight we can all get together and discuss our options."

14

As Arlen Behr waited outside Lee's tent, he could see that Ken and Dan were in deep conversation. He began formulating a plan to insure that his mission would not fail.

15

At dusk, Will and Harry mounted the wagon. Will cradled Haskins' book in his hands, while Harry grabbed the reins. They watched Nelson for the go sign to ride through the thin membrane separating 2013 and 1863. A lump came to Harry's throat; not from fear, but from anticipation of being able to see the past unfold through his very eyes, and the opportunity to help rescue his brother. Will was a little apprehensive as to what it was going to feel like going through that thin membrane into the past. Nelson was busily looking at the time feeds from the past, seeing the sun finally begin its descent toward the horizon through Ken's eyes. He walked over to the wagon, and grasped Will's hand, then he walked around the wagon and then took Harry's hand in his, squeezing it. "This could be really rough, my friend. Dan is protected by Lee, but you..." Nelson choked up.

'"It's okay. I'll keep my cool and I'm sure Will should have something to say to General Lee about seeing to my protection while we're in his camp."

Nelson nodded, and let go of Harry's hand. He stepped away from the wagon and gave a hand signal to one of the technicians. The tech flipped a couple of switches and tapped in a command on his keyboard. The threshold to the past was now open.

Harry worked the reins, nudging the mules forward. They slowly walked toward the shimmering opening in the rock face, becoming a little skittish as they saw the image of green cascading water growing larger and larger. When the mules' snouts passed through the hole to the past, their bellowing and snorting abruptly stopped. The animals were virtually disappearing a few inches at a time until he was holding reins apparently attached to nothing. A moment later, he looked down and saw his shoes begin to disappear, followed by his legs, outstretched arms and finally the rest of his body. He glanced to his right, and saw the look of wonder on Will's face. They turned their heads and saw the rest of the wagon begin to emerge from the green transparent hole. Nelson stood inside the facility, along with techs busily going about their work. As soon as the wagon passed completely through the time portal, it disappeared, turning into solid rock, a tangle of trees and brush standing sentinel in front of their only entrance back to their time. He pulled back on the reins and stopped the mules.

Will opened Haskins' book and flipped through the pages. Every word the Confederate Corporal had written 150 years ago had survived the journey to 1863. He showed the book to Harry. "The book made it intact, man. Now we better follow our instructions to the letter and locate markers that will guide us to this exact spot, or else we might not be able to get back."

They dismounted the wagon and looked for natural markers before going to the task of fashioning markers that would blend in with the natural landscape. Harry noticed a solitary pine tree standing conspicuously by itself about ten yards from the wagon. He walked over and stepped off the distance from the tree to the rear of the wagon and wrote the information on a slip of paper. Will searched the opposite area, noticing a tree with a large knot clearly visible on its trunk. He stepped off the distance and wrote his information on the paper.

They mounted the wagon and as Harry urged the mules forward, Will kept a visual on the two natural markers. As they proceeded, he wrote down more information about the landscape until they finally came upon a rutted road. Many wagons had gone this way. Both men searched the terrain for markers and the sight of a large boulder not more than three yards from the far side of the road was Harry's reward. "I think this rock will certainly suffice as a natural marker to guide us back to the exact point we have to be in order to return to the future. If we can conquer the many extremely difficult challenges we are bound to face, the mission could be an absolute success. I can't wait to see my brother..." He saw Will frowning. "What's wrong?"

"You're going to have to dumb it down some. In 2013 you are a well-educated man, but here in 1863 you're just a..."

Livid with what he was hearing from his friend, he pulled back the reins and lashed out. "A what, Will? A dumb nigger! Yes, sir, Massa! You be so right dat dis nigga not look or talk smart. I be 'zactly whats you want me to be." His paused, his anger subsiding. "Trust me, man. I know what I have to do, but that really stung me coming from someone I would give my life for."

He nodded. "I'm so sorry for even saying that. I know you will do what you have to do to convince the Rebs that you are a free man working for me."

He took the reins and got the mules moving down the road toward the Confederate camp

16

Back in the TTF, Nelson viewed the confrontation between his two friends. He was certain Harry would handle himself well and he dismissed any possibility of the Confederates believing otherwise. He turned his attention to another scene. Sergeant Arlen Behr was returning to his post to guard Dan.

When Behr accidentally killed Sergeant Stewart, Nelson had great cause for concern and was considering scrubbing Will and Harry's entry to the past.

17

Earlier, after Behr arrived at Lee's tent, he spoke to the sentry. "General Lee wants me to wait inside his tent."

The guard, knowing that this man had killed a fellow Confederate soldier, looked at him with pure contempt, but nodded and pulled the tent flap aside. Behr walked in and strolled behind the desk. He rifled through some messages, quickly noting the contents, and under the pile, he saw a book and picked it up. When he saw the date of publication was 1871, he began flipping through the pages, skimming each one as he quickly went about his work. When he came to the first blank page he was confused but he continued to thumb through seeing blank pages to the very end of the book. He placed it back on the desk and sat down to ponder this discovery.

18

General Lee pulled back the tent flap and stepped inside. Behr immediately stood, came to attention, and saluted the Confederate commander. After returning the salute, Lee softly said, "Please sit down, Private Behr." He then walked around his desk, noticing the pile of messages lying there. He sat down and stared at Behr for a few moments. "Have you looked at anything on my desk, Private?"

"No, sir. I would never do anything like that."

Lee considered the answer and nodded, believing he was being truthful. "I am greatly concerned with the death of Sergeant Stewart and I want you to tell me exactly what happened." He sat back in his chair and locked his hands in front of his stomach.

Behr looked the general dead in the eyes. "Sir, before you left camp, Sergeant Stewart approached us as we were guarding General Rodin and threatened to hang him..."

Lee abruptly stood up. "Why wasn't I told this earlier?" He was totally outraged at this news.

Behr shifted in the chair. "Sir, I guess we figured we could handle the situation and didn't want to get you involved. I see now that we made a mistake by not notifying you immediately. I am truly sorry, General."

Though still agitated, Lee sat down and calmed himself before speaking again. "You are correct. You two men did make a great mistake by not informing me, but because General Rodin is still alive I will not mete out any punishment. However, I strongly suggest you keep me aware of anything concerning General Rodin. Do I make myself clear?"

Knowing the suggestion was clearly an order, he replied, "Thank you, sir. May I continue?" After Lee nodded, he continued with his story. "When you left camp, we could see that Sergeant Stewart was enlisting the aid of a number of his friends and when I saw them heading up toward us, I told Younes. We decided we'd have to level our rifles at the small mob as a show of keeping to our orders to protect the ni... general."

Lee's eyebrows rose but he allowed him to continue.

"Sergeant Stewart grabbed my rifle and pulled before I was able to take my finger off the trigger. The rifle fired and now a fellow soldier is dead. I wish I could be able to go back in time to stop what happened."

"That's an odd statement to make. You know you can't go back in time and undo what has already been done." Lee suddenly became lost in thought. *I say this yet I want to do the same thing. I want to undo the result of this war to suit my needs and preserve my country.*

After a few moments he heard Behr say, "Sir, are you alright?"

"Yes, thank you. I believe your story but I want to speak to Private Younes shortly. Please escort him and General Rodin back here and then take the general to his tent. Keep him under guard until you are relieved."

Behr stood and saluted. He then left the tent and walked back to the tree.

19

"Arlen, how did it go? Did Lee believe the shooting was an accident?"

"Yeah, Ken, he did, but I think I might have made a mistake. I told him I wished I was able to go back in time to prevent the shooting and after I said that he seemed to go into a brief trance. Man, I hope I didn't blow our covers, even for a minute letting him think that we could be time travelers. When I was alone, I took a few moments to rifle through some papers on his desk and I came across a journal written by Private Haskins." He looked at Dan. "General, can you tell us what this journal is all about."

Ken put his hand on his friend's shoulder. "Dan told me about the journal and I didn't have time to fill you in, but I think the only way we can keep the course of history intact is to watch over Haskins and hope that he writes exactly what he is supposed to write to fill the blank pages. As far as what you said about going back in time was a slip of the tongue for sure, my friend, but maybe he won't think any more of it. We really have to watch what we say."

He nodded. "Lee wants to see you in his tent while I take General Rodin back to his. I sure hope I haven't created a serious ripple in time by shooting Stewart, but I guess we won't know that until we return to our own time."

Younes reported to the Confederate general with a hand salute. "Sir, Private Younes reporting as ordered."

Lee returned his salute and offered him a seat. After they were seated, he looked at the soldier thoughtfully and asked, "What exactly occurred out there?"

"Sir, may I speak freely?" Lee nodded. "Earlier today, Stewart and another soldier approached us as we were guarding General Rodin and he told the general that he hated niggers and was going to lynch him. Private Behr and I went along with his comment because we felt that if we would go against him, he'd really get agitated and try something at that time. We hoped we'd gain some time to figure out what to do to protect the general and ultimately, I guess we were wrong. One of us should have come to you immediately. Later, when he gathered some strength in numbers, I was really worried because I was sure the mob was definitely going to hang General Rodin and we'd be in a great amount of trouble with you. I am truly sorry, sir for not coming to you earlier."

Lee pondered this for a few moments and said, "When I spoke to Private Behr, he said he wished he could go back in time to stop what happened. That, of course, isn't possible, is it?"

Younes sighed, perceptibly, and replied. "Of course that isn't possible, sir, but I guess all of us have thought one time or another that we could relive a bad incident in our lives so that it would not have happened."

Lee nodded. "You are correct, sir. I have probably thought about that on many occasions during the course of this war. Do you think the Confederacy can win this war?"

Without missing a beat, he smiled. "Damn right...excuse my language, sir. I truly believe the Confederate States of America will survive for a long time. I've had my fill of the North trying to impose their will upon us and I will fight to the death for what I believe in."

Lee smiled. "Son, I hope you are right. I want this war over, but not at the cost of our freedom. I believe you are a good soldier and the matter of Sergeant Stewart's death will be considered an accidental shooting. Thank you for your honesty and now you are free to go and continue guarding General Rodin." When he began to shuffle through some papers, Younes stood up and left the tent.

20

Nelson Wainwright paced the floor of his office, waiting for some good news. After Behr shot Stewart, he put the girls to work to find out if Stewart died at Gettysburg. The techs checked history books and didn't notice any major changes, but that didn't mean that something could have happened over the last one hundred and fifty years since he died.

He watched the tape closely, hoping Saundra's suspicions were totally invalid, but he recalled noticing something about the man's eyes that got him thinking her qualms could be true. Fast forwarding, he scratched his head, watching Ken step into Lee's tent, seeing much concern in the general's eyes. His secretary paged him over the intercom "Dr. Wainwright, there is a call for you on line three." He hit pause and picked up the phone. "Wainwright."

"Dr. Wainwright, its Saundra."

He swallowed the lump in his throat and felt bile rising from his stomach even before she continued. In the past, he had relied on her sixth sense. As they watched the situation with Behr unfold, she told him that she had a bad feeling about Behr, but she couldn't put her finger on it. "Go with your gut and check it out, then," he told her. Now he knew the news wouldn't be good. "Yes, Saundra. What have you discovered?"

"I checked every source I could find, and came up empty. Then I called Behr's wife and asked her if any of her husband's ancestors served in the Civil War. She told me that his great-great etcetera grandfather Lucian served in the Confederacy under General Longstreet. I thanked her and looked up his name but there were no entries. I decided to see if the name Behr was derived from another name and when I checked the name Behren, bingo, there he was. After the war he became a hardened man with a lot of hatred toward the Yankees. He was accused of murdering three former Union soldiers. Enroute to prison, he managed to escape. The reason this never showed up in the background check was because when he settled in Georgia, he changed his name from Behren to Behr."

"That's outstanding. Thank you so much."

He hung up the phone and once again began to watch the drama unfold in 1863, knowing there was only one way he could get that information back to Younes. He was paged again.

21

Will and Harry rode into camp, an escort on horseback leading the way. Numerous fires were lit, casting a good deal of light on the approaching wagon. Soldiers, curious as always, needed to see what was going on, and many of them edged closer to the wagon, seeing an elderly white man and another nigger sitting on the seat high above the ground. Both time travelers heard the grumbling and verbal taunts directed at Harry and they thought for sure a riot could ensue as the angry soldiers edged even closer to the wagon, grabbing the reins of the horses to stop the wagon on the spot.

One soldier yelled, "What the hell is this nigger doing in our camp?"

****

Inside his canvas prison, Dan smoked a cigarette and tried to figure out how he was going to keep the course of the war running in the right direction. As he thought hard, he heard a commotion outside. A couple of mules were braying and a voice said, "Whoa, mules." Dan stood at the open tent flaps and looked across the open space, the light of the campfires glowing brightly. He suppressed a smile. They were here.

Harry stepped down from the wagon and was immediately approached by a couple of Confederate soldiers sniggering and mumbling racial epithets. Will stepped down from the other side of the wagon. He grasped the hand of a young soldier. "Howdy, soldier. Me and my man have brought you all some food to keep you strong when you all go out to battle to kill some more blue bellies."

As some of the soldiers eyed up the other black face in camp, Robert E. Lee stepped from his tent after hearing the noise. Harry nearly made the mistake of coming to attention in the presence of the great man, a man he always respected as he studied the history of the Civil War, and now he was staring straight into his eyes. He smiled and grasped his hand. "Suh, it be a great pleasure to meet a man as great as you be." He shook his hand vigorously.

Lee, though a bit shocked by the informality of this man, couldn't help but laugh, which brought on a great many stares and dropped mouths from the soldiers in hearing range. "Thank you." He looked out toward the assembled crowd of soldiers. "Men, this man is working for someone who has provided us with a great deal of food and he shall also be treated as well as General Rodin while he is in this camp. I will not tolerate anyone who belittles him because of the color of his skin, and to guarantee that he is not harmed, he will billet with the general."

He turned toward Will and offered his hand. Will took it and said, "Thank you, General Lee. I am a hardworking man, but I don't think I could make it without Harry. He has been a hard worker and because of his labor, we have managed to have a profitable farm. Oh, sir, I am so sorry, my name is Will Jennings and the food I have brought you and your men should help sustain you for a couple of days. I only wish I could have brought more."

Lee nodded. "My men and I thank you and your man for what you have brought us. However, I question why a farmer from the North would want to help us in the fight against your country."

"Sir, I was raised in Virginia, but in my travels, I came upon the piece of ground I now own and knew it was where I wanted to live and grow my crops. This area has such fertile soil and I have had many good harvests in the twenty years I have lived here. When the South seceded, I considered going back to Virginia, but chose instead to stay here. We made many trips south to give a portion of our harvest back to the people of Virginia, although were nearly caught a few times by Yankee patrols. It is an honor to serve you and your men."

"Thank you, again, Mr. Jennings. I will have a few of my men help you set up for the night and your man will be safe in the tent with General Rodin."

"This General Rodin, sir, is he under guard because he violated your orders? I have never heard of a general officer under guard in all my life."

"Mr. Jennings, it is a long story, much of which I will not speak, but General Rodin is a Union general and he is black. That's why he is under guard."

Will, playing the game, acted stunned. "The Yankees have a black general! My, my, that is something I never thought I'd hear. I understand that black soldiers fight well, but to be promoted to general with their lack of reading, writing and speaking skills is truly amazing. Would it be possible for me to meet him and satisfy my curiosity?"

"I will allow you to talk with him. After you prepare your quarters, have one of my men take you to his tent. I know you are a civilian, not subject to the laws of the military, but if he tells you anything that seems..." he paused for a few moments, ..."out of the ordinary, please do not discuss it with anyone but me."

"Sir, if he gives me information about the Yankee army, I will certainly bring that to your attention." Lee nodded and then walked back to his tent. Will and Harry began unloading the wagon, with the help of some soldiers. After Harry helped Will set up his sleeping area, they both were escorted to Dan's tent.

22

After Nelson spoke with his wife, he met with the top people in the TTF. "I had a call from my doctor and the news isn't good. I only have about six months to live." He saw jaws drop but before anyone had a chance to speak, he raised his hand to keep them silent. "I haven't told any of you about my cancer because I didn't want my health issues to deter you from your mission here. I have just spoken to my wife to tell her my plan, and although she was saddened, she approved, now knowing what had to be done to keep the Civil War timeline intact."

He looked at shocked faces because they were all sworn to secrecy, although more than a few of the people in this facility shared the secret with their spouses. "Now knowing that Behr could try to change the outcome of the battle and ultimately the war, because of his ancestry, I felt that the only way we have a shot at keeping things normal would be for me to make the trip back in time. I don't want to jeopardize the life of another soldier, but someone needs to try to go back there and get a message to those men in the past."

Nelson paused for a sip of water. "I will pass through the wormhole tomorrow morning. I know I may never see any of you again after I leave and I want to say that it has been a great pleasure working with you all." He paused briefly, gathering his thoughts, and then decided there was nothing else to say. He turned and departed the room through a back door leaving the staff to talk among themselves, even though they all knew that Nelson would never change his mind.

23

After the tent flap was closed, Dan hugged his brother and then Will. Tears came to his eyes and in a low voice he said, "I thought I would never see you guys again. Tell me everything you know. I am sure they won't give us much time together, but we do have security with Ken and Arlen standing guard, so brief me."

Will's smile turned somber. "Dan, there is so much to tell you about what is happening back in 2013, but what's going on here is much more important right now, so I'll focus on those things and then if we have time, I'll clue you in on the Time Travel Facility. The photo that was taken of you has never appeared in any books published during and after the war, so perhaps nothing will change from you being here.

"Since we've been in the loop, we have been watching you from the facility and listening closely to what has transpired. When Nelson heard about Haskins' book, he went to work finding out if there were any more copies in existence. One was found and we brought it along with us. All of the pages are intact, so we know what he must write. Nelson is hoping that if we can get him to write his entries in advance, the events may unfold properly, but we don't know for sure, because of what Lee knows."

"Yeah, I pretty much figured that since he got more out of me than I really wanted to give him, that information alone could allow him to make changes to history no matter what we would do to prevent those changes."

The tent flap opened and Ken stepped inside. "Guys, you have to keep it down a little. We could hear every word you said and if anyone else is in ear-shot there could be trouble." He closed the flap before anyone had a chance to respond.

In a more hushed tone, Harry said, "What do you think would happen if we all went to Lee and told him we were from the future? Would that be enough for him to stay the course that has already been written?"

Dan shook his head. "I've only been here a short time, but from what I have seen of him, I think it would take a great deal more to convince him. I think you guys are right--the book is the answer to the problem."

"This might really sound farfetched, but what do you think would happen if we could smuggle Lee to 2013 and have him see for himself what the future holds?" Will searched the other's eyes, waiting for their input.

Dan's eyes opened wide. "Is that possible?"

Harry nodded, shrugging his shoulders at the same time. "Brother, earlier this evening, a man from this time period passed through the thin membrane that separates our two time periods, so we know that people from this time can be sent to the future. We don't know if they can return to their time because the man, a Confederate soldier had been shot and the doctors were working furiously to save his life."

After lighting up a cigarette from one of the fresh packs Harry brought with him, Dan said, "I guess sending Lee to the future could work, but can you even imagine what could happen back here once his men find out he is missing? Also, what would happen if he couldn't be returned to 1863? I, for one, don't think we should even attempt it. The answer to keeping the future intact has to lie upon the shoulders of the five of us and Corporal Haskins."

Ken roughly opened the tent flap. "Your time is up. Mr. Jennings."

"Thank you." He turned to Dan. "General Rodin, it was a pleasure meeting you and I hope I will be able to talk with you before I leave camp.

As Will stepped out, General Lee stepped in. "Daniel, I want to apologize for what nearly happened to you in my absence today. I also want to ask you to not discuss certain things we have talked about with, um...Harry. My men are not happy that there are now two colored men in this camp and I have warned them not to attempt any kind of foolish behavior, but I don't know if I can guarantee your safety. I am placing a guard at the rear of your tent as well as the two guards in front. In the morning we will talk again."

He stepped back outside without waiting for any kind of response.

Harry hugged his brother again and spoke to him in a near whisper. "I don't know how the hell this could happen, but you aren't the only one trapped in the past. When Nelson took us to the TTF, we saw that there are three other involuntary time travelers stuck in different time periods in history. They've been stuck there for up to eight months and no one has discovered a way to return them to the future."

"Well, that certainly doesn't sound promising at all. I guess it's possible I could be stuck here until I die, but how will that affect history? I'm not supposed to be here. My mind is just spinning. I think I need to get some sleep and see what tomorrow brings." Dan stretched out on the ground and closed his eyes.

Harry looked at his brother for a few moments and then he followed suit. He was pretty sure that no matter what happened, they were going to be in some Confederate soldier's sights before too long.

June 29th

1

Dan felt a hand on his shoulder and immediately reacted by grabbing it and pulling the person down to the ground, straddling him and grabbing his neck with both hands.

Ken Younes coughed and croaked, "Dan, it's me, Ken."

He let go and got off him as Harry woke up to the sound of Ken's voice.

Ken sat up and in the darkness began to speak. "We have a problem."

"What's going on? I am so sorry for what just happened. I guess my military nerves are still pretty good." He clicked his lighter and lit the lantern.

"Yeah they are. You're still strong as hell too. Behr is gone and he must have taken Haskins and the book with him. Will woke me a couple of minutes ago and said he was knocked out and when he regained consciousness, he lit a lantern and found his things had been gone through and the book was missing. I looked around the back of this tent before coming in, and Haskins wasn't there. I don't know what this all means, though. I remember a couple of years before we were assigned to the Time Travel Facility, he told me that his great-something-grandfather fought in the Civil War, and I guess he must have fought for the Confederacy. What other reason would he have by kidnapping Haskins and taking the book? He wants to change history." He slapped his thigh in frustration.

"What time is it?" Dan inquired.

Ken pulled a pocket watch from inside his jacket. "It's 4:47. It'll be dawn pretty soon. I don't think we're going to be able to get out of here before daylight, so if we're going to go hunting for them, we'll have to wait until tonight. Hell, we don't even have a clue where to begin to look for them."

"I'm guessing that Behr is going to find a spot for them to hole up during the day and not venture out too much, even though this area is crawling with Reb soldiers, and they would pretty much go unnoticed unless Haskins would shout out to someone. I think the first thing we need to do is to try to find out if they lit out on horseback or on foot. I don't know if they take inventory of horses every day, but if any are missing, I'm sure General Lee will hear about it soon enough. When he also finds out who is missing, my guess is that he'll come to us to see if we know anything about the disappearance of two of his men." Rodin lit a cigarette and stretched his muscles.

"I just remembered that Behr told me his ancestor fought with Longstreet. I'm betting that they headed for his camp. Old Pete just might believe any story Behr will feed him."

"You might have something there. The question now is, do we approach Bobby Lee and tell him you and Behr are from the future, here to protect me, or try to get out of camp and catch them along the trail somewhere. The other question is if Behr doesn't have the book, who does?"

The tent flap opened and Will stepped inside holding a cloth against his skull. The cloth was blood stained so Dan jumped up to check out his wound. He pulled the cloth away and a little bit of hair along with some skin came off with the cloth.

"Damn, my head hurts like hell."

As Dan looked him over, he made him count the number of fingers he held up and then he moved his hand in different directions to see how well his friend could follow them. "I think your eyes are okay and you'll probably have a nasty lump, but otherwise you should be fine in a couple of days. What exactly happened?"

He sat down on the ground and winced. "I had to go outside to take a piss in the middle of the night. I came back in my tent and was ready to go back to bed when I heard the canvas tent flap being pulled aside. Before I could turn around to see who it was, something, probably a pistol butt, crashed into the side of my head and I dropped like a stone. I only came to about a half hour ago and saw that my pack had been emptied and the book is missing."

Ken chimed in. "Haskins is missing too, and so is Behr. We figure that he heard that you brought a copy of the book from the future and that it survived the trip intact. Behr had an ancestor who served in this war, with Longstreet. I think he's gonna try to rewrite history through the journal, which will then be automatically transferred to the book."

Will nodded his head in agreement. "What are our options to get them and the book back here?" He looked directly at Dan.

"We could try to get out of here at nightfall and try to find out where they went. Ken thinks that they may be headed for Longstreet's camp to try to convince him to help change history, or as he said, simply have

Haskins write an account every day that will probably change the course of events as they were first written. I just don't know. I'm also thinking that perhaps taking Lee to the facility could help to keep the battle on track. After he sees what the future is like, he may stay with the course of the battle as he would normally do so, instead of second guessing himself. No matter what course of action we take, it's possible that none of them could work."

"I don't think we could convince Lee to go to the future, but if we reveal that we are from the future, and what has gone down here in the past half hour, he may be able to figure out a way for us to leave before sunrise. Let's face it, guys, if we don't find Behr before he has Haskins write in his journal, we could all be dead meat."

****

Dan stood up. "So what do we do, Ken? Just have Lee join us and spill the beans? He'd have four people who could give him Intel about the battle. He'd change the course of history for sure." He stared at the men in the tent, waiting for a response.

"That's so true." He paused a moment. "Sorry, guys, I'm fighting some pain in my head. Lee is a control freak. If we explain the situation, he just might buy into letting us go find them."

After a few moments of silence, Ken spoke. "How 'bout I go to his tent and tell him that someone attacked Will. Will was disoriented and found his way over to me to tell me what happened. He collapsed outside this tent and I dragged him in before reporting. I think Lee would come here and then we could tell him everything. He might suffer from a little bit of info overload, but four men from the future could fill his head with the idea that we could summon thousands of men with modern weapons to support the Union lines. Lee could never win, and he would lose most of his army in a matter of a few days. If he believed that, I think we'd have a pretty good shot at him keeping to the course of the war, and let us find Behr before he does something really stupid."

The other men nodded and Ken left the tent to get Lee.

2

Less than an hour ago, Nelson was awakened by the ringing of the phone. He picked up. "Yes!"

"Doctor Wainwright, please turn on your monitor. We have a situation developing."

He hung up and grabbed his remote control. Corporal Haskins was sleeping peacefully when Behr approached him. Behr awakened him by placing the tip of a bayonet against his throat, covering his mouth with the other hand.

"Corporal Haskins, you and I are leaving this camp right now. Don't make a sound."

Wainwright sat straight up and was now one hundred percent awake.

Through Behr's eyes, he saw Haskins being led from the tent and they walked into the woods beyond the camp's perimeter without a soul seeing them leave.

He stood up and watched them walk into the darkness until they couldn't be seen anymore. After he got dressed he walked into the control room and grabbed a cup of coffee. He was debriefed by the lead tech and a little later the screen split and he saw the powwow inside Dan's tent. After the conversation ended, he strode to the clothing room, and picked out the outfit he would wear on his trip to 1863. His papers were ready in case he needed them. He was fairly certain Ken's idea would work, but they still had no clue how to find Behr and Haskins, even though the Time Scope was able to track them using heat signatures. Going back was the only way he could get the information back to the men so they could find Behr and Haskins. Nelson would have to wait, though, to see if Lee could be convinced and then to see which direction his people would go. He took his time dressing, feeling a little frightened and euphoric at the same time.

3

After Ken was escorted into Lee's tent to tell him about what happened, the great Confederate general slipped into his boots. The two men walked to the tent and Lee stepped inside while Ken waited outside to keep watch. Lee saw Will holding the side of his head as Dan and Harry sat still, waiting for Lee to speak.

"Mr. Jennings, what in blazes happened? Private Younes told me you were attacked and robbed. Did you see who committed the crime?"

"No, General, I didn't see who gun butted me, but I know who it was. Sir, it was Private Behr."

Lee sat down on the chair that had been left inside the tent for his visits. "How do you know it was Private Behr?'

Will stared at Lee, formulating his thoughts. "Ken, can you hear us okay?"

From outside the tent, Ken replied, "Loud and clear, Will."

Lee toyed with his beard. "What is going on here?"

"Sir, I know how difficult it must have been for you to accept the fact that Dan is from the future." He paused momentarily to let his words seep into Lee's brain. When the general looked at him with a furrowed brow, he continued. "Harry is Dan's twin brother and I am one of his oldest friends. Ken and Behr are sergeants in the United States Army in 2013.

They were sent from our Time Travel Facility to watch over Dan. Harry and I arrived to try to help them find a way for Dan to escape so that we could all go back to our own time. Now, sir that will not be possible until we are able to find Behr and Haskins, and stop Behr from forcing him to alter his historical journal."

Lee stood up. "This is preposterous. True, I have come to believe that General Rodin is from the future, but the way he explained it, his arrival here was due to a quirk of nature. You speak as though people in your time can pass freely through the corridors of time any time you please..."

"General, would you like to take a tour of our facility?"

Lee's mouth opened, but no words came out. He sat back down on the chair, hard. "You could take me to your time?"

Will nodded. "If you see what we have accomplished perhaps you wouldn't be so set on winning the upcoming battle and perhaps the war. Should the Confederacy win, it is quite possible that we might not be born. A Confederate victory could prove disastrous for not only the United States, but for the whole world. Could you live out your life knowing that what you are trying to do could cause major damage to the time stream as we know it? Countless lives of people from 1863 until the end of time could change..." He felt a catch in his throat and could no longer speak.

Lee sat quietly, rubbing his temples. He sighed and locked eyes with Will.

Will took a deep breath and spoke quietly but firmly. "General Lee, you are a soldier, a great leader of men and one of my heroes." He let that sink in for a moment. "In 1971, we three were serving our country in a little country called Vietnam. We were ambushed as we moved toward an enemy stronghold. If Dan had not reacted as he did during that battle, the three of us would probably have died that day. He was awarded the Medal of Honor for his actions and I was so glad we were all able to go home and live wonderful lives until he was thrown into the past. I don't want that to change. He not only saved our lives, but the lives of at least fifty men because of his quick reactions. I am begging you, sir, to allow us to get out of here and track down Behr and Haskins before a man from my own time creates havoc with not only this time, but everyone's future as well." He sat back down.

Robert E. Lee stood up and raised his voice, "I still believe that the Confederacy can win this war and that our actions could make the world better. I do believe that I must let you men find your man and my soldier and stop them, but the decisions I make on the battlefield will not be influenced by anything you say."

****

Upon hearing this, Ken stepped inside the tent. "General Lee, I must warn you that the TTF could send thousands of men to this place and this time to join the Union ranks. We have weapons that you cannot even imagine, and there is no way you and your people could ever win this war. An action of that magnitude would alter many lives, but the United States must be preserved at any cost."

They all stared at him as if he had lost his mind, but suddenly Lee seemed so deflated, believing every word he said. He stood up. "I suggest you all leave before the sun rises and find those two men. Any decisions I make from today on will be mine and mine alone. I will confer with my generals, but ultimately, I will be the man to give the orders. May God be with you!" He stepped outside and ordered a corporal to gather all the men outside his tent. He was going to create a diversion.

****

"General, I have to ask you one more thing."

He turned and looked at Dan.

"We think that Behr is going to try to get to General Longstreet's camp. What is the fastest way to get there?"

Lee stepped back in the tent and told them what direction to take, and nothing more. He stepped back outside and walked toward his tent.

4

In the TTF, Nelson watched the verbal exchange with great interest. He nearly spit out his coffee when Ken told Lee that thousands of men with modern weapons could be sent back to 1863 to assure a Union victory. The amount of power to accomplish such a mission would be astronomical and he didn't think it was a good idea to even try it, but the statement certainly grabbed Lee's attention.

He turned to a technician and asked if they knew exactly where Behr and Haskins were and he was answered with an affirmative. The two men were heading directly toward Longstreet's camp.

"Are our people heading in the right direction and how far behind are they?"
"Sir, they are on the correct course they're about two miles behind."

"Will you be able to get me close to our men?"

"Yes, sir. You'll be able to pass through the portal and be within fifty yards of them. They will also see the portal opening and know someone is coming from here."

Nelson patted her shoulder. "Good work. How soon will I be able to go?"

"We'll be sending you very soon. Are you sure you really want to do this, sir?"

He responded with a nod.

Ten minutes later he was stepping through the rock wall into the past.

5

When Robert E. Lee assembled his men, except for a few guards, the men from the future made their escape into the woods behind the orchard. The sun began to lighten the sky as the four men started walking in the general direction of Longstreet's camp.

Ken, who was on point, signaled for the men to take cover and they all dropped to their bellies, hugging the ground, exposing as little of their bodies as possible as a Confederate patrol passed by not more than twenty five feet from where they hid. After Dan, who was the last man in line, was certain that the patrol was out of sight, he stood, with the other men following suit.

"That was close, guys. I know we have to keep moving, but we are really going to have to be careful. If the Rebs see us with two black men, they are going to be more than curious and our mission will be doomed to fail. Failure is not an option." He saw the men nod, although Dan and Harry seemed to be a little shaken. That was certainly understandable.

Ken took out his compass to make sure they were going the right way. He was almost certain that Behr probably gagged Haskins so he couldn't shout out to any Rebs in their general vicinity, and they might even have gone to ground until nightfall. He took a bearing on a rocky ridge and was stunned when he saw a green glow and Nelson Wainwright step out from the Time Travel Facility.

"Gentlemen, I presume this isn't Oz?" He felt surprisingly well after traveling 150 years in an instant.

They all laughed at his joke as he shook everyone's hand.

Dan was so glad to see him, he gave him a hug. "Dr. Wainwright, it is a pleasure to meet you. Harry and Will filled me in on the facility and what you guys and gals do. I certainly hope that you are here to give me the news that you found a way to get me back to our time?"

"Well, there might be a possibility, but our first job is to find Haskins and Behr. We can't allow them to get to Longstreet's camp. Behr's ancestor, Lucian Behren, is there and I know he wants to meet him." He spread a topographical map, circa 1860 on the ground and pointed out where they were in relation to the camp.

"The camp isn't too far from here..."

"They have about an hour lead on us; do you think we'll be able to intercept him in time?" Ken interrupted.

Nelson glared at him for a moment, hating when someone stepped on his toes, but he cooled off. "I know you have a lot of questions, but please let me finish before you ask." Ken realized it was not a request and simply nodded.

"Just before I stepped into the past, I was given their present location. They are holing up because Behr is waiting for nightfall. He obviously knows we were listening in to his conversation with Haskins, but he doesn't know that he can be tracked by his heat signature. My greatest fear is that if he sees any of us, he'll shoot first and ask questions later, so we have to be cautious.

"He told Haskins that they were supposed to find General Longstreet and tell him everything about the journal and Haskins bought it. I have to assume that as soon as they were out of earshot of Lee's camp, Behr probably bound his hands and gagged him so he could neither get away nor shout out to any patrols they might spot. Questions?"

"Yeah, Dr. Wainwright, I have one," Dan inquired, "Because of my appearance in 1863 has the future been altered in any way? I don't even know if you can answer that but I had to ask."

"That is a good question, and please call me Nelson. We've checked the history books against our data base and nothing really sticks out. I imagine you're concerned because of Sergeant Stewart's death by Behr's hand. He died in the battle of Gettysburg, so his death earlier is probably inconsequential, unless he saved someone who might have died, and that could ripple, but we won't know for sure until the battle is over. There could be wrinkles eventually, but, again, we'll have to check that out later and we can't worry about it too much now."

After taking a drink of water, he continued. "Also, I told you that there may be a way to bring you back to 2013. A Confederate soldier stumbled into the facility. He was researched and was listed as MIA. It's possible that we could transfer you and him at the same time, but he's still not out of the woods. He was shot but he is recovering. Again, that's a problem we will deal with when the time comes. Once we capture Behr and get Haskins back to Lee's camp we're going to come back here to try the transfer. I can't make any guarantees, though." He put his hand on Dan's shoulder. "Any other questions?"

The other men shook their heads, but Wainwright could tell that Ken had something on his mind. He'd probably ask later. "Good. I brought some food, so I suggest we eat and get a little rest before we move on."

6

Hiding behind an outcropping of rocks, Behr scanned the immediate area and seeing no patrols, he took off Haskins' gag.

"Where are you really taking me, Private Behr?"

"I'm really taking you to Longstreet's camp, Haskins. There is someone there I have to meet, so before we report to 'Old Pete', I'm going to stash you for a while until I finish my business. No harm will come to you if you do everything I say." He gagged the man once again.

After making sure that his prisoner was not too uncomfortable, he picked up his rifle and set out for the camp. He wanted to meet Lucian and talk with him. After all, how many people could say they talked to a great something grandfather nearly one hundred and twenty years before they were even born. As he walked, he blazed his trail so as not to lose his way back.

7

After Ken utilized the map and shot an azimuth with the compass, the four men from the future set off to find where Behr and Haskins were hiding. They all realized that it was possible that they might not find them, but they had to try. All of them knew what the stakes were in this manhunt, none of them wanting their futures to be changed. After wandering through some thick brush, they came to a swampy area where Ken saw the footprints of two men. These prints had to belong to Behr and Haskins because there were no other prints nearby. Who else could have been walking through here recently? Probably no one.

He took another compass reading using the direction of the tracks and they set off again. About a half hour later, they came upon an outcropping of rocks and Ken raised his hand, signaling a halt.

He turned around and the others walked toward him.

"Dan, I think those rocks would make great concealment. Don't you?"

"Absolutely. My gut tells me that they are definitely there. I suggest you and I come around from the east while Will and Harry come around from the west. If we get behind them, we might be able to catch Behr with his guard down."

Will spoke up. "I agree with you wholeheartedly. You were seldom wrong in Vietnam and because of that, you saved a lot of lives. Let's do it."

Will and Harry gave Dan and Ken some time to get to the east end of the rocks and as soon as they started heading north, they followed suit, walking very slowly and carefully to stay concealed and make no noise. Fifteen minutes later they saw Haskins, sitting on the ground with his back against a large boulder. He was gagged and appeared to be sleeping.

Ken and Dan saw the same thing from their vantage point. Behr was nowhere in sight, but they agreed they would wait a little while longer before approaching Haskins. Behr could be in the woods urinating or looking for water. After fifteen minutes passed, Dan figured that Behr was not going to be back anytime soon. He may have taken off for Longstreet's camp by himself, but he couldn't figure out why would he leave Haskins tied up and gagged? He raised his hand and signaled Harry and Will to move in. When he saw them moving, he and Ken did the same.

All four men were hovering over Haskins. He was sound asleep. Dan leaned over and lightly shook his shoulder. Haskins' eyes flew open in both surprise and fear, until he realized his captor was not present. The he relaxed when Dan removed the gag and untied his hands.

"General Rodin! Private Younes! What are you doing here and who are these other men?" He kept looking from Dan to Harry and back again, obviously noticing how much they looked alike. He also seemed to be both frightened and bewildered as Ken offered him a drink of water from his canteen.

Now would come the difficult part. Dan sat down beside him and put his hand on the young corporal's shoulder. "Andrew, you kept looking at Harry and I and saw a resemblance." He waited for this to sink in for a moment, then Haskins turned to him with a confused look on his face. "Andrew, Harry is my twin brother. The other man is Will Jennings. Both of them are from the future and have come back here to attempt to return me to my own time."

Haskins' jaw dropped. He looked pleadingly toward Harry and Will and they both nodded, reassuring him that Dan was telling the truth. He closed his eyes for a few moments and then opened them, hoping he had only been dreaming, but the truth was staring him in the face. He looked toward Ken.

"Private Younes, tell me I'm dreaming and that I'll wake up soon?"

"Corporal, you are not dreaming. I am also from 2013. Behr and I were sent back to 1863 to protect General Rodin and keep history, as we know it, intact."

Haskins was shaking his head. "No, no! This can't be." He momentarily accepted the truth when Will and Harry nodded to him, but now he was shaking with the impossibility of it all.

Dan comforted him and when he calmed down, he looked at the four men from the future, nodding his head. He had been crying and wiped the tears on the sleeve of his gray jacket.

"Andrew, where is Private Behr?"

"He tied me up and gagged me. Told me he was going to General Longstreet's camp to see someone and then he'd be back."

"Did he take your journal with him?"

"No, General! He left everything here stashed behind some bushes. He only took his rifle and both of our canteens."

"How long ago did he leave?" Ken inquired, offering him a piece of smoked meat.

Haskins chewed gratefully for a while and after he swallowed he said, "I think he must have left about an hour ago, but it's hard to say since I didn't know the time when we got here. Best guess I can make."

"Did he say anything to you about who he was going to see?" Ken wiped some sweat from his brow.

Corporal Haskins merely shook his head, not knowing anything more.

They'd have to wait there until Behr returned to find out what he was up to.

8

General Lee was still digesting everything he had heard in the past two days; he had slept fitfully last night, images of a battle circling around in his head, with many thousands of his men lying dead on the killing fields. He stood by the table gripping the edge tightly, tears flowing from his eyes and wetting his moustache and beard. He sighed heavily knowing that Dan was right. He had to stick to the decisions he would make because no matter what, he was still the commanding general and if he seemed weak, his staff would know something was wrong.

He was informed that last evening, a spy named Harrison rode into Longstreet's camp and informed him that when he was in Tarrytown, Maryland, about fifteen miles from Gettysburg, he saw large numbers of Union troops moving north and he felt that they would come very close to Confederate forces. Longstreet was apprehensive about the believability of this man, but he was told that Harrison's information was usually quite reliable. Longstreet rode to Lee in the middle of the night with the information supplied by the spy. Lee was skeptical because he had Jeb Stuart out looking for the location of Union forces. Longstreet urged his commander to trust in Harrison's eyewitness report and Lee decided he must get his army together and prepare for a battle very soon.

He read reports from the field and was in the process of writing new general orders when his aide stepped inside the tent, clearing his throat to get his attention.

Lee placed his pen back in the inkwell, looked up and waited for him to speak.

"Sir, I am here to report that General Rodin has escaped. The two men who came in on the wagon last night, Corporal Haskins and Privates Younes and Behr are also gone..."

The general jumped out of his chair, interrupting, "Who was guarding General Rodin last night and didn't anyone in this camp hear or see him escape?" Lee brushed by the aide and strolled toward Rodin's tent.

He felt bad. He gave the men permission to escape, but he had to pretend that he knew nothing about it. He would have to punish a few men to keep up the façade and he hated lying and deceiving.

Later, as he listened to his men explain how the escape occurred; he was lost in thoughts, wondering about the future. If he would see those men again, he would definitely ask them for a tour of their Time Travel Facility.

9

Dan sat on a rock under the broiling sun. The sunshine felt good on his skin and he was truly hoping that somehow he would be able to get back to his own time very soon.

Will and Harry sat down beside Dan. He smiled at them wearily.

Will took something from a pocket and placed it in his hand. "Thought you might want this back, General."

He was surprised being called General. His friends still called him by name or LT. He opened the pocketknife and ran his finger over the blade. "You took some time to sharpen it for me. Glad you found it. I hadn't left it out of my sight until I dropped it a hundred and fifty years from now."

Will chuckled. "LT once I stepped on it and saw that it appeared to have been left there long, long ago, I had a feeling that somehow you had gone into the past. When Nelson contacted us and told us that time travel was a reality, it blew my mind. To be back here and see the actual men that made history, is pretty overwhelming. I was absolutely enthralled meeting General Lee."

Dan started whittling a piece of wood he picked up from the ground. The knife slid through the bark easily and soon he had clean wood to work with. "Yeah, he is quite a man. I don't know if I got through to him but I guess we'll find out over the next four and a half days, till the battle is over. If everything that is supposed to happen will. I hope Nelson and Ken catch up with Behr and stop him before he does anything stupid to jeopardize the recorded outcome of this war."

10

They had followed Behr's trail for over an hour, hoping they would catch up with him, but fearing that they wouldn't.

"What do you think he's gonna do when he meets up with his ancestor, Nelson?" Dan inquired.

"I don't know, but I'm afraid that he might say something or do something that would have serious consequences in the future."

"What if nothing changes? Is that possible?"

Nelson pondered this for a few moments before answering carefully. "It is possible. The other people trapped in different times in our past haven't created any alterations to our time, but they've been controlled very well by the people we sent back to help them stay out of trouble, for lack of a better term. The travelers and their TIs have intermingled with folks from those time periods with no ripples or butterfly effects occurring so far."

"I understand that. Ever since we've been able to transcend time, we've always been afraid to do anything that could have that effect. I remember when we took classes and the instructor explained the butterfly effect. He told us that the term stated that if a butterfly flapped its wings in South America, it could change the weather in Texas. That seemed a little farfetched at the time, but since we've been coming back, I can see how the effect could work."

As they continued to discuss the effect, they saw Behr step out from a copse of trees pulling up his pants.

****

Dysentery had done its job. Behr was disgusted having been in the woods crapping his guts out. After three bouts of diarrhea, he lay down and fell asleep. He woke up feeling the urge to go again and two more bowel movements emptied him out. He cinched his pants with a rope belt and picked up his rifle. Looking to his left, he saw two men waving to him and he recognized them.

11

Back in the TTF, the three ladies from research, Saundra, Steph and Mel had watched Nelson go back into the past. They were still amazed with how the process worked and that they were able to see what he saw. Hearing his voice was also still pretty unbelievable, as it was to everyone who worked there. Some of the most intelligent people in the country were stumped as to how seeing and hearing people in the past occurred. It was something that was being studied every day since the first time traveler walked through the green haze to another time and place.

Saundra was concentrating on a monitor showing the man who had been whisked back to New York in 1930.

He looked toward the Time Inspector walking by his side. "I sure do miss home, John. How soon do you think the facility will be able to get me back? What is my wife going through since I went missing two months ago?"

"Sam, I wish I could tell you something but when I went back yesterday to refill your prescriptions, they still had no idea how to retrieve a traveler who was sent back to the past by other means than through the facility. Betty is doing okay, dealing with you being gone, but she misses you a lot."

His head dropped toward his chest. "I miss her, too. Perhaps a solution will be..."

Saundra heard Steph and Mel scream and she focused in on the large monitor just in time to see Behr level his rifle and fire, hitting Nelson in the shoulder. As Ken looked after him, Behr continued on to Longstreet's camp at a run.

****

Nelson was turning pale from loss of blood and Ken applied pressure to the wound trying to stop the bleeding. After a short time, the bleeding stopped but Ken knew he'd have to get the bullet out to save his life. He pulled a clean piece of cloth from his pack and laid it on Nelson's chest. Then he took out his pocketknife and sterilized it by running it through the flame of the lighter, now happy that he did bring a few necessary items back from 2013. He gave him a piece of leather to clamp his teeth on and then dug the bullet out and poured whiskey into the wound. Nelson grimaced but he didn't scream. Ken bound the wound with the clean cloth and then gave the doctor some water. He let him rest, watching Behr run over a hill until he was out of sight.

12

The brothers and Will heard the distant shot and immediately ran toward the sound. Several minutes later they saw Nelson walking with his arm over Ken's shoulder. Ken was supporting him with an arm wrapped around his waist. He looked very pale and Harry spotted the bloody bandage covering his shoulder.

When they reached the two men, Dan and Will took Nelson and laid him on the ground as Harry began to tend to his wound.

Ken took a huge gulp of water and proceeded to tell his friends what had happened.

"I don't know why he shot Nelson, but he must be in Longstreet's camp by now and I just have a feeling he's going to tell ole Pete who he is and where he comes from. This whole shooting match could change very quickly and not for the better, I'm sure. Harry, how is he?"

Harry looked up. "He'll make it. You did a good job getting that ball out of him and stopping the bleeding. He's going to have to go back, though, or I'm afraid he might have complications without more meds and a proper hospital stay."

"We're going to have to get him back to where he came to the past and hopefully we'll all be able to go through and back to our own time. Chances are that I and more soldiers will have to return." Ken said, and then he took another drink of water.

Dan touched his arm. "Do you think I'll be able to go back with you guys?"

He shrugged. "I don't know. From what Nelson said, it seems like you won't be able to go back until the soldier trapped to our time is healthy enough to send back. I think I'll go through with Nelson to see if they will be able to try a retrieval with you. We're just going to have to wait and see."

Dan turned and walked away from the men from the future. He was so morose not knowing if he'd ever make it home again. As much as he wanted to walk through that green membrane that separated the past from the present, he was afraid. *What if I got stuck in some kind of limbo, never to exist in any time frame? What if I began to walk through and just disappeared forever?* He rolled his head around a few times to help release the tension he was feeling. He just didn't know what would happen. He'd been a soldier for over two-thirds of his life and in that time he'd been scared shitless, but during each mission only three things could happen-he'd come out unscathed, wounded or dead. Being trapped in time was more terrifying than anything he had ever imagined because being here could change so many lives. He had no control over the outcome.

Harry let his brother have some alone time and then he walked to him. "Will and I have decided we're going to stay here with you for however long it takes to get you back to 2013."

Dan smiled and grasped his brother's hand. "I can't let you guys stay here. You have families to take care of and I don't..."

"There's no arguing, brother, we're staying."

Dan stared at him intently, his anger rising, yet he tried to stay calm. "Absolutely not. You are going home and you are going to live your life for as long as you have to live. I refuse to allow you to stay here with me. I will be fine and someday they will get me back. I have never asked you for anything before, but I am begging you to please go home."

Harry nodded and after shaking hands and hugging his brother, he walked back to the others.

The men lifted Nelson from the ground and began walking back to where he had arrived from the future.

June 30th

1

After a fitful night, sleeping on the ground, Dan awakened to the sound of numerous horse hooves galloping his way. Not wanting to be seen, he entered some thick brush and laid on the ground until the soldiers passed by. When Ken didn't come back to the Time Travel Facility, Dan figured he had no chance of retrieval. When the window to the future opened, Dan could see inside the facility. He was so close to changing his mind. He wanted to return home so badly but he held his ground and watched as first Ken and Nelson, then Will and finally Harry returned home. As soon as the four men were back in 2013, the portal closed and once again became a rock wall.

When the patrol was out of sight, he decided that he was going to head to South Mountain and try to hook up with some Union troops. He was pretty sure that Behr really screwed up and told Longstreet that he was from the future and knew how to change the course of the war. He fervently wished he could find Behr and shoot him himself.

2

Yesterday Behr ran hard and fast, waiting for a bullet to tear into him and the further he ran the more he realized that he had to go back and accept whatever punishment would be meted out to him. He was pretty sure he hit Nelson in the shoulder, not a fatal wound by any means, but he would surely have to go back to the facility to get the proper medical attention.

Taking Haskins and going to Longstreet's camp to see his ancestor to try to talk him into not killing any Union soldiers after the war was over was totally senseless and selfish. His family suffered a stigma for a long time, and he hated the man who ruined the lives of many people.

Talking to Lucien would be so wrong: attempting to change the future to suit his own needs. That went against everything he was taught. He stopped running and turned around. He became a little disoriented and could not find his way back before night fell. He slept in a copse of trees, knowing that he would take his medicine and live with the consequences of his actions.

Once again finding his way, he felt so much better about himself and lost in his thoughts he never knew someone was approaching him from the rear until he was knocked to the ground.

He hit the ground hard with his left shoulder and his rifle was knocked out of his hand. He saw it bounce twice before Dan Rodin picked it up and pointed it at him. Ken Younes pulled him up to a standing position and made a threatening move with his fist but stopped himself.

"Why in God's name would you shoot Nelson, Arlen?"

He stared at Ken and then at Dan, who was still pointing the rifle at him; he had even pulled the hammer back so Behr knew he had to be very careful with what he said or he could wind up dead. "I shot him because I was afraid you would get a shot off at me before I would be able to get to Longstreet's camp. I took off in a run and then the realization hit me that I could not do what I was planning on doing and I had to come back and let the chips fall where they may. I slept in a little copse of trees a couple of miles from here."

"So what was your plan? Were you going to alert Longstreet and try to change the outcome of the Battle of Gettysburg?"

He shook his head. "Could I please have a drink of water?"

He handed him the canteen: he drank his fill before handing it back.

"Thanks. No, I was going to tell my ancestor all about what he was going to do after the war and how it would affect my family from that point on. I wanted to get rid of the stigma that man gave us by shooting those Union soldiers after the war ended." He looked into Ken's eyes. "I never wanted to hurt anyone, but I was so tired of living a lie. We had to change our name from Behren to Behr so people wouldn't know what he had done."

Dan slowly released the hammer disarming the rifle and placed it on the ground. He lit up a cigarette and inhaled deeply. He looked at Ken. "How is Nelson doing and what are we going to do now? Chances are we're going to run into Rebs marching toward Gettysburg and we don't have much firepower if we have to shoot our way out of here."

"He'll be fine. After the portal opened and we all went back to 2013, I took the opportunity to grab a shower and get a good night's sleep. I brought back some food and cigarettes for you. I didn't want you going it alone and figured we had to stop Arlen one way or another."

He put an arm around Arlen's shoulder. "Telling Lucian who you are could have created unbelievable changes to the future. Somehow we have to insure that nothing changes and I figure the only way we can do that is to get to the Union lines, and help fight the battle if necessary."

Dan listened quietly, trying to formulate a plan of his own when Ken asked, "Why didn't you want to try to come back through the portal? I think the soldier that was shot would certainly want to change places with you when he is strong enough."

Looking up, he replied, "That's probably true, but I gotta admit that I am scared shitless about trying to get back to our present by any other means then the way I came to be in this time."

"What if you can't go back that way, and what are the chances of that freak storm happening again? I think if you don't try retrieval at some point, you might be stuck here forever." he replied in a soft voice.

Dan shrugged his shoulders and then raised his head when he heard a horse bray not too far away. "They're coming guys, we gotta hide now!"

3

Late yesterday afternoon they operated on Nelson. The doctors debrided the wound, cleaning it out, finding slivers of metal and removing them. He had been given antibiotics and had spent the last twenty hours or so sleeping.

4

Will and Harry were watching the action unfold in 1863 on the large monitor; occasionally glancing at the smaller monitors fascinated by what was going on with the other people trapped in time.

Harry was not happy leaving his brother behind in 1863, but he knew that Dan had a good reason for not wanting to try to enter the portal to the present. He didn't know what the reason was and that was the one thing that pissed him off about his brother. He very seldom shared his thoughts when he decided to do something that concerned both of them or friends. Vietnam changed him in many ways, one being his openness to share and no matter what Harry tried, he could not crack that shell with anything.

Will knew that Ken sent them back because of their ages. Even though he and Harry, and Dan as well, kept themselves in very good shape, running around in the past was probably not a good idea. He did really enjoy the short period of time he spent there and meeting Robert E. Lee nearly took his breath away. If he was thirty years younger he would volunteer to be a Time Inspector in a heartbeat.

Both men, though deep in their own thoughts, continued to watch and listen to the people that were trapped in the past.

"I guess I can understand why Behr shot Nelson. He and his family must have suffered greatly after their ancestor murdered those Union soldiers," Will said.

"Yeah, I guess I can understand too. Fortunately the weapons Ken and Arlen carried were technologically enhanced to be extremely accurate. I do believe Arlen only intended to wound Nelson, but I am afraid he might inadvertently do something that could create ripples. What do you think will happen when he comes back to 2013?"

Will shrugged his shoulders, "Good question. I imagine if and when he returns from the past, he could face a court-martial."

"Yeah, let's hope nothing happens to him back there, or there could be changes in our time. However, since these events have already occurred, can they be changed?"

"I wasn't sure of that before we came back yesterday, but I've been giving it a lot of thought and I have come to the conclusion that the book, actually only a journal in 1863, is not magic. I think since it has already been published it can't be changed. My gut tells me the only factors that can change the course of history would be a death that should not have occurred, or perhaps a life saved. What effects those occurrences would have, I would have no idea.

"I would also venture to guess that if Lee makes different decisions, history could be changed, but my guess is that his decisions will not change. I think history will stay intact, and I just want our people back home as soon as possible."

He turned his attention back to the monitor in time to hear Dan say, "They're coming." He could also hear the horses in the distance.

5

The three men from the future scrambled into a patch of brush alongside the trail, just as three riders came into view. Unbelievably they were Union soldiers and if Arlen and Ken were seen in Confederate uniforms, they, and Dan, would probably be taken prisoner. The riders pulled back on the reins, stopping, and then Dan saw the reason why: Arlen's rifle was lying out in the open, and one never passed by a weapon without picking it up.

He clenched his fists. He just totally forgot about the rifle and now a real big problem could occur. When a soldier picked up the rifle, he would notice how much lighter it was than a musket from this time. A .58 caliber musket weighed in at about nine and a half pounds, but the replica, now being picked up by a private, weighed a little over five pounds. Dan saw the private heft it with a quizzical look on his face. "Do you think we can take them, Ken?" he inquired.

"I don't know, but if we don't and that musket gets inspected further, there could be problems down the road."

"I have an idea." Dan smiled and then slithered out of the brush and walked right over to the three soldiers who were now dismounted, looking over the musket the private was holding. He had told them that it must be a new weapon because it is so light.

After they all hefted the weapon, Dan came right up to them, drawing their attention away from the musket.

The soldiers looked him up and down; curious about why a black man would be out here alone and also taking good hard looks at his unusual clothes. They had their rifles at the ready, but Dan was playing the stupid card, not speaking, and smiling like Davy Crockett trying to grin down a bear. He reached into a pocket of his fatigue jacket, causing one of the soldiers to bring his rifle up a bit, but when he produced a fine looking cigarette and lit it, the soldier lowered his weapon again. He blew smoke toward them and he was sure that it smelled better than anything any of them had ever smoked. He reached into his pocket again and shook three cigarettes from the pack and gestured for the soldiers to take them. They did and laid their weapons down as they lit up. Dan was smiling and nodding his head, which Ken and Arlen took as a signal to approach the Union soldiers.

When they were sighted, one of the Union soldiers made a move for his musket.

Ken raised his specially made musket, pointing it at the soldiers. "Howdy boys. How ya all doing today. It's a nice day for a ride. We'll be needing your uniforms, your weapons and your horses, but we will allow you to keep your canteens. So if you will please strip we'll be getting on our way real quick like." He smiled and nodded his head at the men.

As the one soldier took off his shirt he said, "You all won't get too far. A lot of our boys are on this side of the mountain over yonder and I expect you sure can't go back to your own lines, having this nigger with you. You're sure to get shot. Now if you allow us to take you prisoners, you'll be treated well and probably will have a good chance to live long lives." He smiled at his captor.

"Well, that sure is a nice offer, Corporal, but I think we'll take our chances. You boys might find yourself prisoners of the Confederacy because soon, there will be a large force coming this way. I suggest you head north and maybe you'll miss out on all the slaughter."

No more words were spoken and when the three Union soldiers were stripped down to their skivvies, Ken said, "Okay, boys we're going to leave now. Much obliged for the uniforms, horses and weapons. The papers you were carrying might come in pretty handy as well." He kicked the horse's flanks and the three men trotted east toward Gettysburg, not knowing what they were going to do next.

6

Nelson watched the scene play out on a monitor that was brought into his recovery room. His blood pressure rose significantly along with his heart rate. He was livid and finally shouted out, "What the hell are those guys thinking, especially Ken. Taking everything from those soldiers except their skivvies and leaving them where they could be found by Lee's soldiers could really have a devastating effect on the outcome of the battle to come." He squeezed his sheet tightly in his hand and began to cough and gasp.

A nurse and a doctor came into the room as soon as they noticed his blood pressure and heart rate climb to a near dangerous level. The nurse adjusted the flow of his IV's to help bring the rates down as the doctor pressed a stethoscope to his chest to listen to his heart and lungs working.

Their appearance diverted Nelson's attention from the drama in 1863.

"Nelson, you can't get too excited or you're going to harm yourself further."

He smiled. "Doc, I don't think my outburst is going to make my cancer spread any faster than it is already. You are a man of medicine and I am a man of science. Scientifically the problem back in 1863 is much more grievous than my impending death. Now, I don't know what to do, Blaine. It's bad enough that I allowed Sergeant Younes to return to the past, but with Sergeant Behr making the decision to kidnap Haskins and then wanting to tell his ancestor who he was, I really had no choice but to allow him to go back and keep an eye on Behr and protect General Rodin." He sighed and closed his eyes shaking his head from side to side.

Blaine McAllister placed his hand on top of his friends. "I don't know what is going to happen either. Ever since you brought me in on this project after Alicia died, I have been overwhelmed with this whole notion of time travel. I accept it because it is fact, and when people get sent back in time by other means than through this facility I know you have to send people back to keep those rouge travelers out of harm's way. So even if the scenario in Gettysburg turns out without any changes in history, what is to stop those other people from changing history where they are at?" He grasped Nelson's hand and squeezed hard.

Nelson shrugged his shoulders. He knew his friend was right and that any other time travel incident could cause mammoth ripples in the fabric of time. Perhaps he just needed to let go and accept the fact that the three men in 1863 would do all they could to preserve history. He'd just have to wait and see what happens. He closed his eyes and slept.

7

After riding for about a half hour, they took shelter in a patch of woods. Ken handed out energy bars, instructing Arlen and Dan to not leave any of the wrappers on the ground. Until they had a chance to make a fire, they'd have to carry the trash with them.

Arlen, with the energy bar dangling from his lips like a cigarette, looked at the blue uniforms putting each top against his chest and the trousers against his legs, trying to see which one would fit the best.

Ken laughed. "Where do you think you are, man? Joseph A. Banks! None of the uniforms will fit us like gloves but the three Union soldiers were pretty much the same size as us so any shirt and pants should fit you."

"I know. I just have a habit of looking at all my clothes in this manner before I put them on. The last time I was in a barracks, I took out two BDU tops, both camouflage, and alternated holding them against my chest. Out loud I said, "Which outfit looks better on me, the camo or the camo. Three pillows were fired at me in rapid succession."

Dan roared. "Yeah I remember a guy in basic training. He was a real hippie before Uncle Sammy's Green Machine grabbed his young ass. He adjusted quickly to military life and he was looking in his locker prior to formation and said to me, 'I think I'll wear this nice green outfit today, Dan.' It was just so funny at the moment I almost pissed myself laughing so hard." Then his smile turned into a frown. "In Vietnam, he was killed with only four days left in country. Damn shame the losses in that fuckin' war."

Arlen finally decided on a uniform and it actually fit him pretty well. "Our mailman used to talk about Vietnam a lot. He had a pretty safe job in Saigon working in the Embassy, but his life changed when the VC attacked in '68. He was scared shitless because an enemy soldier was no more than ten feet from him but luckily didn't spot him and he survived. I read quite a bit about Tet and it was pretty amazing that the Communists didn't take over the city. I read that the 716th MP Battalion pretty much saved the city. Must have been hell." He looked at Dan. "You were infantry?"

He had his pocket knife out and was whittling again. "Yeah. I was a lieutenant back then. Will and Harry were in my platoon so not only did I have to worry about forty to fifty guys, I also had to watch out for my best friend and my brother."

Ken chimed in. "You and your brother served in the same platoon? I didn't think they allowed that back then. I thought the army didn't want to have to notify parents that two brothers died together."

"That's true. I thought you heard Will tell Lee that yesterday. The only exceptions were when brothers volunteered together. Our parents weren't too happy about it, but they knew they wouldn't be able to talk their stubborn boys out of going over there and getting their asses shot off. We had some really close calls, but we made it home." His voice softened. "I sure hope I can make it home from here."

"Maybe we ought to rest here and try to hook up with some Union cavalry tomorrow. If my recollections serve, I think Buford's cavalry will be on this side of South Mountain sometime tomorrow morning. There's going to be a lot of movement, so we're really going to have to watch out for anything. I suggest we ride out at dawn."

Both nodded and they made themselves as comfortable as possible. Dan said, "I'll take first watch."

July 1st

1

A few minutes before the sun came up, they saddled up. Ken and Arlen were wearing two of the stolen uniforms while Dan was wearing civilian clothes that Ken had brought back to 1863. He was also carrying papers declaring him a free man. The TIs possessed papers that identified them as Union soldiers. All the papers had been forged in the TTF to help give these men a better chance at survival. They rode in silence, having to duck into some trees when they heard approaching horses; the Confederates were on the move heading toward Gettysburg.

Shortly before 6am they were a little northwest of the city when they were halted by Union pickets. These men were part of cavalry under the command of General John Buford. One of the soldiers spotted the three men on horseback and jumped to his feet shouting, "Halt, who goes there!"

They halted their horses and raised their hands. Ken shouted, "Don't shoot. We're Federal troops separated from our company. I'm Private Ken Younes, the other soldier is Private Arlen Behr and the free black man with us is Daniel Rodin. There is Confederate infantry a few miles behind us. We saw them and had to hide in the woods to evade capture."

The soldier nodded and ordered them to dismount and come on over. After he called for an officer, Lieutenant Jerome Michaels strolled on over and took a good look at all their papers. He turned toward his men. "Looks like we have a couple of more soldiers to help thin out the Reb ranks. Don't know what we're going to do with the ni...black man, but he is now in our care." He turned toward Dan. "I guess I could put you to work helping to load rifles. Would that suit you?"

"Oh, yes suh. That be real good work for Dan. I be a real fast loader and if you need me, I can shoot, too. My ole Massa used to take me hunting wit him and he taught me to shoot. Sometimes he would get tired and I do all the hunting. Shot a couple of deer and lots of rabbits." When he smiled, everyone laughed.

Dan felt the minie ball pass by his right ear and saw Lieutenant Michaels's face disintegrate. His body stood for a few moments and then crumpled. Dan fell to the ground, pulling the lieutenant's pistol from his holster and turned to face a large group of Confederate soldiers. He had six shots and he was going to make them count if he needed to fire. His military training nearly had him pull the trigger and then he stopped himself, not wanting to change the future by killing a soldier. He would use the weapon to protect himself, though.

He looked around and saw that all the men had taken whatever cover was available. He vigorously shook his head when Ken and Arlen looked at him and the weapon in his hand. He pointed to the weapon and again shook his head. They understood and nodded.

2

Nelson was up and about. His shoulder hurt like hell, but he could not bear to lie in that damned bed anymore. He didn't have much longer and he wanted to accomplish whatever he could in the little time he had left.

As he watched the monitor he was so relieved that the bullet missed Dan but he cringed when the lieutenant was hit. It was the most horrible thing he had ever seen and he hoped he wouldn't see any more, but he figured that would not happen, not when the battle was beginning to escalate. Men were dropping on both sides. The images seen through the eyes of those men were more than even the toughest soldier inside the facility could bear.

The sounds of men screaming literally bounced off the walls and three female and one male worker had to leave the area because they were crying too hard to do their jobs. Nelson understood and just let them go but he would have them return very quickly if more people were needed.

Saundra came out from her office and walked over to him. She tried not to look at the monitor, but she couldn't help herself. After watching for a few moments she turned toward her boss. "Lieutenant Michaels was killed on July 1st, 1863, so there won't be any changes to history as far as he is concerned. All the data we have retrieved so far show no apparent changes to history."

"Thanks. I think you ladies need to take a break. The three of you have been at it for over four days with very little sleep. Hell, none of you have even gone home and I do appreciate it, but there will be more long days ahead. I know you won't go home until this is all over, but I am ordering you all to find empty beds and crash for at least four hours."

She kissed her boss on the cheek. "Okay, Nelson. I know we are all tired so we'll obey your orders and take a break. See you this afternoon." She turned and walked away.

He watched the action for a few minutes until he heard his name paged. "Doctor Wainwright, please report to Doctor McAllister at your earliest convenience."

Reluctantly he headed for the medical facility.

3

There was a lull in the fighting so Dan scurried over to Ken and Arlen's position. Men were screaming and groaning. The stench of blood and gunpowder permeated the air. The dense smoke from the firing of many weapons was beginning to dissipate but his eyes were raw and red from the acrid smoke.

"How are you guys doing?" he inquired, reaching for the canteen of a dead soldier. The soldier had taken a round in the stomach and his guts were spilling out on to the ground. Flies were already having a field day on the corpses and comatose wounded men. He took a sip of tepid water, but it helped relieve his parched throat.

"I'm okay, Ken said, looking over the carnage, "I threw up some a little bit ago, but there's nothing else in my stomach. The dry heaves are getting to me though."

Arlen nodded. "I'm good, too, but I've never seen anything like this, even in Afghanistan. It's hard not shooting back at the damn Rebs though."

"Yeah, I know." Dan slapped at a fly that was biting his cheek. He didn't realize that he had a lot of the lieutenant's blood on him. "We have to try not to shoot anyone because we don't know the havoc it may cause in 2013. If I recall correctly, we'll soon be pulling up stakes and heading for Little Round Top. Buford knew that holding the high ground would be paramount to a Union victory. If we do that, at least today's battle should be following history pretty closely.

"General Lee will be riding this way shortly, consolidating his forces to dislodge the Union troops as quickly as possible. He will set up north of Cashtown Road and direct his troops to strike on three sides of the Union defenses. By the end of today the Union defense will take the shape of a fishhook starting at Culp's Hill and running up Cemetery Ridge and ending at the Round Tops. A lot of mistakes are going to be made today which will be extremely fortunate for the Union. Hopefully, this battle will stay on track and nothing will change."

4

Nelson opened the door to Dr. McAllister's office. "Hi Blaine. I came as quickly as I could. What's up?"

He looked up from his iPad. "Nelson, you aren't going to believe this, but while you were unconscious we drew blood from you, not knowing if your body chemistry could change when you transcended time. I guess it's something we never thought about doing with the TIs. But they are all one hundred percent physically fit and you aren't."

Nelson sat down and gripped both armrests waiting for even more bad news. He nodded. "Okay, go on. How much sooner am I going to die?"

"That's what I wanted to talk about. We've checked the results of your blood tests several times and, my friend, you are cancer free." He held up his hand. "I can't tell you why, but apparently going back in time somehow reversed the cancer and it is totally gone."

His body shook. "Oh, Blaine! I can't believe it. I'm going to survive. There is so much more to live for and so much more work to do. Thank you so much for telling me this." He stood up and leaned over the desk to shake his friend's hand.

5

Around 12:30, General Robert E. Lee sat high atop Traveller, surveying troop movements through his binoculars. His thoughts turned to General Rodin, who could possibly be in Gettysburg at this very moment. A patrol brought in three men in skivvies and when they told him of being robbed of their uniforms, weapons, and horses by two Confederate soldiers and a black man in strange clothing, Lee had to laugh to himself. The three men were being sent to a prison camp and they would probably survive the war. Lee had considered all the information Rodin shared with him and had come to understand that if he did anything out of the ordinary, it could lead to catastrophic results in the future. He would not second guess himself.

Last evening, just before dark, Corporal Haskins returned to camp and informed him of the amazing green wall of light. The two men named Will and Harry helped Private Younes escort the wounded man back through the wall of light and then it just disappeared. "General Lee, I was totally flabbergasted by what I saw and I know I can never tell another soul. The future must be a wonderful time to live."

"Yes, son, I imagine it is."

Haskins looked his commander straight in the eyes. "Marse Robert, are we going to lose this war?

At that moment Robert E. Lee never felt so tired. He sighed and then answered. "Yes, son, we cannot beat an army that has so much when we have so little. However, we will continue to fight until we can fight no more and then we will go home and continue with our lives. Many, many more good men on both sides will die and that is the horrible cost of war."

"I am proud to fight by your side, sir, and I will fight until this war comes to a conclusion or I am killed." He smiled. Then he grew serious, saying, "I guess I won't be killed though, since I publish a book in eight years."

Lee nodded and then he watched Haskins walk toward his tent. His heart was heavy knowing that the Confederacy would lose the war but if he did not continue on the course of history could be changed by his non-action. It was horrible knowing that the South would lose many more men, some of them boys really, and that hurt worse than any physical wound that befall him. He sat down hard on his bed to try to rest but sleep would not come for a very long time.

6

Wainwright watched the monitor intently. Buford lost a lot of men, but the Confederates were repulsed. Through the eyes the men fighting in the past, he was able to follow the movement of Buford's division and everything was falling into place according to the battle plans that took place on that first day.

As he watched what was going on he was also looking at maps of the Union and Confederate positions.

Buford's division was on the move after General Reynolds had been killed. The Rebs were pressing the attack and large numbers of prisoners were brought in behind the Union lines. He moved his men to the left flank of the Union line where they would watch and fight the enemy should they come that way. He also took up a position on Cemetery Ridge where he could observe Confederate movements and put men where they needed to be. As night fell, his men bivouacked to the left of his position with pickets spread out nearly to Fairfield.

The men from the future were barely speaking to one another, possibly fearful that they might say something that could give them away. Dan was quieter than the other two, although he would talk to some of the men in Buford's command.

The images were getting harder to see because daylight was gone.

Nelson read that by nightfall the Confederates outnumbered Union troops by nearly 10,000. A few hours later, three more Union divisions arrived while only two more of Lee's made it to Gettysburg. Union commander General George Meade now had 68,000 men to Lee's 60,000.

Exhausted, he went to bed.

July 2nd

1

After a restless sleep, Dan woke up shortly before dawn. He heard men coughing, sneezing, and talking quietly in small groups. He winced when he heard a man scream inside a medical tent. As his eyes began to adjust to the approaching sun and through the dying embers of small fires, he saw Ken and Arlen beginning to stir.

Ken awakened and saw Dan staring at him. He scurried closer. "What is going to happen today that will affect our positions?"

"Well, if I remember correctly, Buford is going to be ordered to defend Little Round Top and we'll be moving out early this morning. They are trying to give his troops a little rest after yesterday. We fought for almost twelve hours and I'm sure the division had over a hundred casualties. Today is going to be a very bloody day."

Daylight now covered the area and the men saw a patrol coming in with a Confederate prisoner in tow.

Later, when they were ordered to move toward Little Round Top, there was a shortage of horses. Since Rodin was a black man, his horse was confiscated by a Union soldier.

He wasn't too upset because he wasn't crazy about riding, anyway. Walking and stretching his legs out would be so much better for him. Sometimes the nuisances of the aging process jumped up and bit him in the butt. He had to remember that he wasn't a young man anymore, even though he felt really good most of the time. He exercised faithfully, doing fifty pushups and a hundred sit ups every day. He watched his diet, although the food he had been eating the past five days had done a number on his stomach. He took a brisk one hour walk each day, quite often with his twelve year old dog. Riley looked forward to those walks, but now...

Later, when they set in about a half mile from Little Round Top, Ken and Arlen were able to hook up with Dan so they could have a meaningful conversation about what they were going to do to survive this day.

They surveyed the movement of Confederate troops to their west and south. It seemed like thousands of men in gray uniforms were getting themselves in position to attack and all three thought they would not live through the day.

Already sweating in his woolen uniform, Ken was the first to speak. "Guys, this doesn't look good. I am not totally familiar with what will occur today, but those Rebs look like they're getting ready to kill all of us." He watched them closely, almost able to see the whites of their eyes because they were so close.

"I agree. We might not make it out of here. Maybe when we took those horses we should have ridden far away from here. The facility always knows where we are and they would have been able to open a portal nearby and we could have gone back home." Arlen stared at the mass of Confederates.

"Gee, thanks, Arlen. What about me? I don't have any idea if I can go back though the portal until that soldier from this time period can be sent back here. His wounds might be so bad that it will be days before an exchange could be attempted."

"Don't worry, General. Arlen and I aren't going to leave you out of our sight. We're here to protect you at all costs and that's what we are going to do." He shot Arlen a look of disdain, because of how he had screwed things up already.

"I'm sorry, guys. I gotta admit I'm scared shitless and I don't want to die on this piece of ground. I will do my duty and protect you, Dan."

Dan nodded and went back to watching the enemy soldiers.

2

Nelson had awakened early. He was feeling much better and the pain in his shoulder was now moderate at the worst. He was still very stiff and was sure he would remain that way for some time but he was going to live, hopefully to a ripe old age.

Checking both sets of printouts about the first day of battle at Gettysburg, he saw that everything was pretty much intact. It was possible that some casualties were incurred by time travelers being there, but no ripples had occurred.

He had listened in to the conversations by the three men in the past and hoped that when Private Teague was strong enough to try the exchange between him and Dan, the transfer would be successful and Dan would be returned to the present. If it didn't work, one or both men could be sent to only the Lord knows where. The doctors said that he should be well enough to go back to his time in about twenty-four hours.

He went back to watching the screen. Through their eyes, he saw so many men ready to kill each other to preserve their ways of life. He could almost smell the scents coming from the battlefield; blood, excrement, cooked food, coffee, gunpowder, all mixing together making the most unpleasant concoction one could ever breathe.

3

Later that afternoon, after a tremendous artillery barrage, the Confederates attacked the left flank of the Union line. The smell of death was in everyone's nostrils and raw fear made men do unspeakable acts to other men. The killing fields ran red with the blood of all Americans, now enemies, but destined to someday be reunited under one flag. That day was still nearly two years away, but it would happen.

Firing the pistol he took from Lieutenant Michaels, Dan intentionally missed every man that came into his sights. He still didn't want to take a chance of altering history, but he also decided that he would not die on this battlefield. He was going to make it back somehow.

Earlier, when Buford was ordered to leave the field of battle, they found a place to hide, so they would be able to stay and fight it out with the Rebs, if necessary.

In mid-afternoon they hooked up with a group of men and then headed up to Little Round Top. Dan felt that they would have a better chance of survival up there then here in what was to be known as 'The Valley of Death'.

Climbing up to Little Round Top was a daunting task. Thick with trees and rock ledges, one had to watch his step constantly. Dan saw more than one soldier fall a long way down and had to climb his way back. He desperately wanted to get to the top to see the battlefield in real time. He took a tour in 2008, and surprisingly the terrain hadn't changed much over the past century and a half. Finally reaching the top, he looked down into The Valley of Death and was horrified with the number of bodies stretched out as far as the eye could see. He looked down upon Devil's Den. Union artillery would fire from here until over two thousand Confederate sharpshooters captured it and would utilize this rock formation to fire upon Union troops. Many brave men would die trying to dislodge the enemy from this massive rock formation.

When Ken and Arlen joined him at the summit of Little Round Top, they saw Devil's Den for themselves. "It's amazing, but seeing this now, as the battle is occurring, has rekindled my memory," Arlen offered. He told them about Devil's Den and then he sighed before telling them about The Wheatfield. "I recall reading that over 20,000 men fought there and over 6000 were killed or wounded. Some of the wounded Confederates tried to cross Plum Run creek, but couldn't make it. The creek became known as Bloody Run. I also read that during the heavy rains on July 4th, many of the wounded men that had not been collected drowned when the creek overflowed its banks, red with blood."

Ken pointed to The Peach Orchard. "I remember reading about what happened here. While part of a brigade of Confederates attacked The Wheatfield, the other part attempted to attack the right flank of the Union line. They were met by a barrage from thirty cannons and were cut to ribbons. Hundreds of men fell, many of them without having ever fired a shot.

After that, there was another charge. Confederate General Barksdale led the charge on horseback. It was said that his long hair was flowing in the wind as he waved his sword in the air."

Dan and Arlen waited for him to continue, assuming he needed time to collect his thoughts.

"These charges by the Confederates posed a lot of problems for Union artillery in the Orchard and The Wheatfield. The batteries had to withdraw under a heavy volume of fire from the Rebs. Eventually they were overrun." Ken grew quiet and Dan and Arlen soon knew why.

Less than one hundred yards away several Confederates were taking dead aim on the three men from the future. They fired their weapons simultaneously.

4

Nelson watched the three men for a long time, listening in on the conversation, impressed with the knowledge they possessed.

Less than five seconds after seeing the Confederate sharpshooters, Nelson heard the guns being fired. He was horrified. Three men who did not belong there were going to die and there was nothing he could do.

When the bullets left the barrels of the Confederate muskets, a bright white light enveloped the time travelers. In the blink of an eye they were gone and the monitors in the TTF went black.

For a moment the entire facility turned black as night and then when light returned, Ken Younes and Arlen Behr were standing in front of the time portal, still horrified that they would be dead in less than a heartbeat.

After the shock wore off, and they realized where they were, they were elated, but where was Dan? He was gone.